Now this jungle cat, as any such wild cattish creature, could move more quickly than any man. But when she leapt forward, the whole weight of her body was set in a course to fly forward through the few feet that separated her from Kinch, whereas Kinch had to move his hands but quick inches to catch at her collar and throat. Kinch caught the jungle cat where throat and breast met with both his hands as a man might catch a grain sack hurtling down on him, and he had then the good sense to push her off sharply ere she might claw up at his hands and forearms. In the space of a heartbeat she hissed and spat and lunged again, and again, and yet again . . .

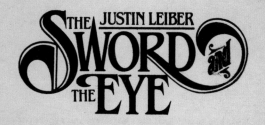

JUSTIN LEIBER

THE SWORD and THE EYE

A TOM DOHERTY ASSOCIATES BOOK

THE SWORD AND THE EYE

Copyright © 1985 by Justin Leiber

A TOR Book

Published by Tom Doherty Associates
8-10 West 36 Street
New York, N.Y. 10018

Cover art by Kevin Johnson

First TOR printing: May 1985

ISBN: 0-812-54429-3
CAN. ED.: 0-812-54430-7

Printed in the United States of America

Acknowledgments are owed to two anonymous balladists, a sentimental Englishman and a somber Scot, and to Eric Rucker Eddison. William Moir, Barbara Strachey, and Derrellyn Yates read and criticized the MS. This book is for Virginia Kidd and Mary Byrd Lloyd.

THE SWORD AND THE EYE

Of arms and a man named Kinch I will tell you.

At my beginning, this Kinch is called "Derwent Holdering," and he is held to be second son of Lord Harold Holdering.

The arms are many—arms are ways of powerful achievement and these ways are many—but there is black war and a sword, a noble singing sword, and a savage beast from far southern lands, and a blind man who sees, and a ruler who is ruled, and an eye and a destiny beyond earthly ken, and many strange men and women both sweet and foul. The arms come before the man, for this is a tale of an action, not a whole life.

Masters and mistresses, the matter is thus.

I

The Dragon Year's tenth full moon hung low over the sea and the southern fens, lighting the harvested fields to the west and north, distantly illuming the sharp crags of Rach Soturn and Rach Soturn Pikes to the northeast, even penetrating the gloom of the Cut, where the sullen sounding sea, now in retreat from fullness, met the river Ham in front of the squat dark fortress. Round about huddled merchant houses, taverns, stables, homes, fishermen's huts, and rude temples of Southkirk.

All was silence save for a dog bark or vivet's whinny and the monotonous creaks of the two mills on the Ham at the northern edge of the town. The harvest celebration of last night had left all sodden with sleep, men's bellies tight with bread and beer, suet pudding and wheaten pasty, meat and wine and even rarer stuff, all according to their station.

The house karls and kitcheners snored all aheap round the slowly cooling ovens, for once as warm and besotted as they could dream of. The great hall slept many tardy guests, of quality ascending from the guild farmers, middle rankers, artisans, master boatmen, and such of the low table to the officers, merchants, sea captains and minor gentles of the high table. The chief gentles and the Vicar's family were long shut abed in the Lord's apartments adjoining the great hall seaward.

The harvest celebration of the tenth moon was grander than usual for it marked two changes in office. In heraldry the first was the fourteenth—the manhood—birthday of Derwent, said second son of the King's Vicar in Southkirk. In no material way second was the solemn installation of veteran Trajus as the Vicar's captain general.

Some way outside the town the stillness broke.

The lips that gave the town's name were rude. They hissed it "South—Kirk" rather than the usual lazy "Sow—erk." Half a league southward, in a grove beside the great southern road that was the last cover before the ford over the Ham, the Lothian general, Lord Sorgun, shifted his saddle-stiff thighs, turning from the two dark-clad and horsed scouts to speak to his staff men.

"Eight of my scouts dismantle the signal fire at the peak on the Cut. And they can hold the peak through to dawn against anything likely from Southkirk.

"Go you and set three score horse over the ford

and spread north of the town. Tell them I'll have their body strings for milady's harp if they fail me. They must stop messengers north while we surround the town. Go!"

As he watched his lieutenants depart into the darkness, Sorgun's hamlike hands pursued a flea through the coarse blond hair that spilled over the gorget of his blackened leather, metal-bossed breast armor to the pommel of his broadsword and his axe. These fall raids on the Salian Kingdom gave fair profit, though there was little glory in buffeting these grain-rich peasant lordlings and greasy merchants until the Salian King paid the Price in portable gold and silver and ilgras. Here he was but ten days on the road and acrawl with vermin.

Perhaps he'd ask one of the priests of the Eye to conjure him free of them. Hah! The pale-skinned flabby creatures would give him dark looks under their cowls and mutter that the Eye was not for karlish tricks. Easier to sorcel the Eye to scorch the world entire than to do some such small service.

Still, it did not do to mock them, even in thought. He held the flea before him unseeing but feeling the plump body ready to pop between the thick, blunt nails of thumb and forefinger. Thus will I soon hold the rich harvest of the Salians, and I am ready to crush the bloody juice from it if the Price come not quick from their king.

So said Sorgun to himself and mashed the flea and lightly shook the reins above his war stallion's withers and ordered his household troop to invest Southkirk.

II

Master Derwent lay dreaming clothed in a linen gown, snuggling under a blanket spun of fine lamb's wool. Very like these were proud dreams, the best sort, woven of yesterday's grand events. His voice had not fully broke from a boy's treble and his height was more that of a gruel-fed house karl, a thin and gawky house karl, than that of a gentle or warrior.

"There's a good five fingers between the fourteenth year and a man's beard," his mother, Lady Edwina, had said to him, smiling gravely as she stretched to spread her fingers over his head. "You will have your father's height, son, and more."

But it was Elgar's height that worried him. Elgar, the first son.

As he slept he could still taste the resinous fourteenth year manhood wine that he had drunk in a

shimmering goblet of silver from the hands of his
father, the Lord Harold Holdering, Vicar of the
King in Southkirk. Heavy, well-muscled, the Vicar
had given him a full warm smile through his gray-
flecked kinky beard.

The Vicar had frowned at him during the installation of Trajus. For at the end Trajus, bright blue
eyes keen as a knife, had turned to the Lady Edwina after doing the oath to the Vicar.

"And to you, my lady," he said softly, for she
was of the Eigin line and his family had served
them as long as folk could remember.

As Trajus bowed to her, his hands came up,
palms over ears as if to represent larger and more
catlike ears. This gesture was made with smooth-
ness and discretion such that most folk marked it
not. But Derwent knew that it was the sign of the
great pard, the fabled lion of the far south that is
the crest of the Eigin house.

"And to him," said the Lady Edwina, her eyes
moving from Trajus to her son Derwent.

"And to him," repeated Trajus, eyes flashing,
and made the Eigin sign again.

It was then that the Vicar saw the high cheekbones and aquiline nose of the demi-royal Eigin line
beginning to emerge in Derwent's face. It was then
that the Vicar frowned.

It was then that the Vicar thought that this Trajus
whom Edwina and her clan had got for him had had
more than a score of years experience as a warrior,
and had journeyed three hundred leagues to the

fabled Southern Empire to learn their military lore. Not so far as to find the fabled great pard, that dun olive monster, sign of Eigin House, that in story outgoes the jungle lynx as the mastiff outgoes the terrier. Yet the Vicar could see in him the rash, overweening fire that the Eigin inspired. The reins must be kept tight on this man, or his resources would be squandered in some foolish adventure.

Southkirk had barely enough horse to mount an hundred warriors. Even a small Lothian host would run through that like a hot poker through a tub of lard. Southkirk was an ill place for maintaining horse. There was little sweet grass and it was boggy throughout save for the ridge on which the town sat and the southern road itself.

With luck they could hold the fort against all but a determined siege. Madness to think they could block the way into the Kingdom itself. As if one could magic the fortress stones to unfold and lengthen, making a wall athwart the road from the Cut to the foothills of Rach Soturn Pikes.

The ruddy fingers of the dawn now fell upon those Eigin marks, the high cheekbones and aquiline nose of Master Derwent, infusing them with a glow that could remind a fearful man of the rumored powers of the Eigin line. There was silence through the fort and the adjoining town. He put off his linen gown, shivering slightly in the cool dawn air, and took up the plate-sized mirror embossed with the figure of the Eigin pard. This was his most costly possession.

He stared at himself perhaps wondering whether
the ritual of yesterday had given him more the look
of a man. Perhaps wondering yet again that his
father the Vicar, brown-eyed, wide-nosed, heavy-
built and boasting much tight-curled black body hair
withal, could have sired him. Certain that the first
son Elgar, of sixteen years and already beyond
common dimensions, was more like to the Vicar.
But Elgar's mother, who died in his birth, was said
to have been brown-eyed and black-haired and withal
more like to the Vicar than the Lady Edwina.

The skin of his whole body was fair with the
lightest fringing of almost invisible blond hair save
for a brown mark that he had discovered just above
his right buttock. Stretching his arm back he could
just see in the mirror the obel-sized freckle, like a
brown rock thrown on a field of snow.

III

Derwent looked through his slit window into the still-dark inner space of the fort. Just below his small chamber in the Lord's apartments at the top of the Keep, the Lord's yard was silent. He could hear someone shouting at the other end of the common yard, where the garrison barracks along the south wall hit the scum grounds. But he could not see. He ran from his chamber up the narrow stony stairs, emerging breathless within the great bartizan of the keep. Looking down from the height of ten men, he could see Trajus buckling his leather, brass-bossed battle harness while he continued shouting brazenly at the main barracks' door.

"Wake and to arms, you sodden sons of whores, the Lothians are in the stables! Wake!" Trajus bellowed and then hurled himself into the barracks.

Master Derwent now looked across the north side

of the fort, past the great hall, the kitchens and the
brewery, where all were still asleep, to the walls
past which the main stables stood. Even jumping to
the other side of the bartizan he could not see the
wooden structures themselves. But he could see the
dark-clad Lothians hurriedly herding away what
looked to be most of Southkirk's horses. This score
of Lothians, uncumbered by armor, efficiently drove
their captive herd north toward the common meadow,
avoiding the homes and buildings that huddled to
the west along the docks and to the east along the
Ham River. Sweat suddenly stood on his fair forehead as he looked farther afield.

On the far edge of the meadow he saw a trio of
lightly armed Lothian horsemen, then two more several tree-lengths to the left of them, a half-dozen
perched on the coastal path, a dozen on the road that
led from the town along the Ham to the great southern road, and then, here and there, wheeling into
position, more than two score were spread, a quar-
ter league away, athwart the farm roads. Even farther north and west, he fancied he saw flashes on
armor or blades of the sun, just risen over the
eastern wastes.

Albeit lightly woven Southkirk was surrounded.
Derwent could taste the richly herbed savory that
he had gobbled at the end of last night's banquet.
For along the great southern road, like a serpent,
stretched a heavily armed host.

The serpent had two heads. One pointed northwest from Ham ford along the great southern road.

Even as he watched this head lengthened and split as several score set on at a relentless pace that would soon have them leagues into the rich wheatlands and agrasp of the peaceful townlets of Moor End, Mirdol, and Mittol, itself halfway to the King's place at Firnis. Surprise and quick seizure was necessary for them, particularly with the Eigin line counseling defiance at court. Surprise. He looked to the craggy peak at the end of the coastal path where the signal fire should be sending warning northward along a chain that stretched all the score of leagues to Firnis. There were no flames.

Now he remembered that last night Trajus, who had first come to Southkirk earlier that day, had asked the Vicar's leave to review the guard. The Vicar, then much drunken, had embraced him roundly and said him nay, arguing that Trajus' office as captain general could only commence with the dawn.

There was congestion where the two heads joined at the ford. There two heavy baggage wagons were being wedged and roped through the ford, where the Ham spread wide and shallowed to a foot and less, though strewn with rocks and treacherous holes. But two wagons for an army of several hundred horsemen. Tents and war gear.

The Lothians fed on the substance of those they raided. And the Price was paid in precious metal. Gold, silver and ilgras. A single horse might bear it.

The other head extended at a slow trot along the

quarter-mile of road from the ford to Southkirk, passing two abandoned farm houses whose beams were still black from the last Lothian raid of two years ago. At the head of this company rode a huge man, dark blond hair coursing from under his helm over his corselet to his waist. Derwent could hear the heavy beat of their hooves.

It had taken Derwent but a few heartbeats to survey the prospect from the height of the bartizan. Below, Trajus, blue-eyed and brazen-voiced, had reemerged, pulling forth a warrior by the neck in either hand. A half-dozen warriors, lightly harnessed but armed, had already come forth. Across the common yard a few of the quality had stumbled from the great hall, scratching and yawning and gawking at Trajus. Through the still inner air of the dark courtyards, Derwent could hear Trajus as he addressed the eight warriors. Trajus' voice was now much lower but the fire and authority in it carried all the way to Derwent. *And to him*, Trajus had sworn to Derwent.

"Now, lads," Trajus said to his tiny troop, "there's one thing we have to do and we have to do it quick as a ferret. Sorgun and his fat Lothians are coming up the road from the ford and his scouts are here and there. And we have no horse. We need to send warning to the wheatlands and the King. Come with me to the postern gate."

Trajus sprang toward the alley that led past the great hall and out the back of the fort. Such was his bearing, so sparked his blue eyes and sword that

the eight followed him. Derwent, though he had not
yet his man's sword, felt like following. He heard
the postern gate shut heavily. Then he thought on
Trajus' words. True, they could nip out before the
Lothians close-circled the fort and town. Returning
would be another matter. Derwent dashed to the
smaller bartizan at the other end of the keep, where
he might view the path that ran by the docks to the
signal peak a half mile to the west, where the Cut
met the sea. There a man might stand on a clear
day and see Moor End and mayhap even Mirdol
across a score of miles of treeless moors and fields.

Trajus had his men at a steady double time.
Faster and they would come on their goal breathless
and divided.

They passed by townsfolk who were hurrying with
a few prized possessions toward the shelter of the
fort. In the closeness of the town they were invisible to
the half-dozen dark-clad horsemen athwart the coastal
pathway to the signal peak.

Surely Trajus knew where the horsemen were, for
he brought his men to a narrow footpath that led
along the sea side of the ridge atop which the coastal
path ran. Scrambling through some scrub and up
the far side, they were past the horsemen and at the
signal peak before the Lothians discovered them.
Trajus and his men hurriedly rebuilt the signal fire
and had it smoking before the Lothians wheeled and
sped up the coastal path.

When the first two horsemen entered the narrow
cut that led the last yards up the rise to the signal

fire, Derwent learned how a long stave with a burning oily rag might havoc a horse, albeit a scouting horse perhaps untested in the line of battle. The second horse reared and turned about, unseating his dark-clad rider who hit the rocky ground one foot still stirruped. The horse galloped full tilt into the others, dragging the bloody mass.

At Trajus' command his men unleashed a volley of darts into the confusion of horses and riders. Another rider fell, rolling through some bracken into a gully. The remaining horsemen hurtled back down the coastal path.

Soon dense black smoke billowed upward from the signal peak. Derwent heard an awful shout below where the Lord Sorgun and his host had come abreast of the fort. As his other men moved close around the fort, Lord Sorgun, his dark blond hair streaming behind him, galloped through the town with a score of his men, scattering townsfolk as a dog might a mess of chickens.

Behind him, Derwent heard a din in the yards as the townsfolk milled within and the newly-risen went to defend the walls. Four bowmen and Elgar joined him in the bartizan. Elgar, the Vicar's first son and already the full girth of a man, looked narrow upon him. "Mayhap you're a man, brother," he said to Derwent, "but lucky for you that Southkirk's walls are high and strong. I'd hate to face the Lothians weaponless and in my nightgown." Elgar laughed, and he strung his great bow and turned to look through a crenel at the Lothians, some a respectful, if surrounding, distance from the walls, others looting the buildings without the fort.

IV

Matters went much as two years ago. Most of the townsfolk without the walls managed to make it within. And those caught out were allowed to hide or slink away. The Lothians did not fire the houses or sheds nor do murderings or rapings, though they skimmed off light valuables, feasted on the choice fresh food they found, and took away the better preserved stuff for their saddlebags. What one asked ransom for and mayhap would again, one did not damage, at least not much and then only to make evident what fate might come if the Price came not. On the block were the many homes and craftshouses of the town, the boats and ships of the docks, and the wheaten harvest, so rich that granary beams bent outwards and great sacks were set up in the open under canvas.

Derwent watched while the defenders shot an

occasional volley of arrows from the walls and ducked
when the Lothian bowmen returned the fire. But
this, he knew, meant little. As before the Lothians
would have little profit and much loss in attempting
to storm the fort, and they lacked the instruments and
patience for a siege. Here Lothians would wait, as
they soon would in the wheatfield townlets of Moor
End, Mirdol, Mittol, and on, most ways to Firnis.
And they would wait with fire ready. And they
would wait not long.

"So eager to be at them?" the Vicar laughed at
Derwent through his tight-curled graying beard when
Derwent asked for his man sword. "Better ask for a
bow. No work for swords now, lad. It'd be folly to
send out our remaining horse. I'll give it to thee
proper when folks gather for supper in the hall."
Derwent had seen to his mother and she had told
him to look for Trajus and his party. But Derwent
went first to inquire after the long grim sword that
was his due. And true it was that such a sword was
for a man ahorse in the open field, not for defense
of a fort.

It was but the second hour before noon when he
returned to the bartizan overlooking the town and
docks. That was when the horror came.

Two Lothian heralds came to the postern gate
bearing flags of temporary truce, black on white.
They came forward cautiously once within bow range.
Another, farther back, blew a horn. The Vicar and
his officers, standing just below Derwent on the
main top of the keep, watched grimly. "Slim trust in

heraldry this," said one. "They come not to the main gate for fear of a sally."

"We bring your wounded," boomed a harsh bass voice. "Let war cease here awhile, and we deliver and you bring them in," continued the herald, giving the ancient formula. "Doth the Vicar, Lord Harold Holdering, agree and agree on his honor?"

The Vicar consulted with those around him. His tall, gaunt elder cousin, Hacmon, then started toward crenels that looked down directly on the heralds, but the Vicar stayed him. "No," said the Vicar, "I shall speak in mine own body, Hacmon. Mayhap that he who brings the bodies would have more converse. The Lothians were not this quick merely to succor our wounded." He strode to the walls.

"The Vicar agrees," said the Vicar. "And on his honor."

Then trotted into sight the Lord Sorgun, the gusting wind swirling his coarse blond hair over his metal-bossed blackened leather breast armor. His huge bulk was but a match for that of his great black war horse. As he came below the walls, he shielded his eyes with one hamlike hand to see, against the sun, who looked down on him.

"And who," he hissed into the silence, "speaks for the Vicar of Southkirk?" And he said the name of the town as two words in the Lothian way.

The Vicar put his foot in the crenel and raised himself so that those below could see his face and chest clear above the merlons. "I speak for the Vicar."

"I see your quality," replied Sorgun, smiling faintly at the Vicar, "and my Lord Sorgun bids you tell the Vicar that he holds him dear and knows that the present difficulty will soon go by, leaving all in peace and amity. There'll be no quarrel more."

"You are to speak of wounded?" said the Vicar solidly.

"Lord Sorgun would have me first tell you of peace," hissed Lord Sorgun.

He glared upward at the Vicar from below his hand. Sorgun's eyes were not the sky-blue of Trajus' but the sick pale-blue of the adder. Though Derwent was some thirty feet seaward of the Vicar, he felt the queasy, engulfing quality of those eyes.

"By what presents does your master know that there will be peace?" said the Vicar.

"By the oracles of the Eye that sees all and tells naught but truth," said Sorgun, intoning the formula of the black-cowled priests.

A chill went through those on the walls. All men knew that the Eye spoke truth when it spoke. And all men knew that to dispute the Eye was like to making the heavens stand still. Yet it did not do to mention the Eye directly unless one were a priest.

"Yet that which sees," said the Vicar, "often speaks riddlewise."

"Assuredly," said Sorgun, "this time it speaks plain as a pikestaff. Despite the pitiful blaze that some fools lit, Lord Sorgun's men will soon surround the riches of the towns north of here. And the Price will come from Firnis well within the limit." Lord Sorgun smiled again but continued.

"Besides," he hissed, "the Price goes cheap this year. It is but half in monies. The rest is but in pay for the prideful Eigin line that hath miscounseled your King against us and our right. The Eigin line is to be anathema, their spawn to be made as the common folk that crawl on the earth. Nameless. And they shall no more see the sight of public day."

The Lord Sorgun then waved his hand, and two horsemen appeared, rapidly pulling a cart behind them toward the walls.

"Here," said Lord Sorgun, his voice rising to a snarl, "I give you as an earnest your wounded and the first casting of the eyeless, crawling, nameless spawn." And Sorgun wheeled and galloped away with the two horsemen who left the cart of bloody bodies beneath the wall. All were clean killed save Trajus, whose eye sockets were empty bloody indentations and whose hamstrings, severed through between heel and calf, poked out like white cords amid the skin, slowly oozing blood. Mercifully, he was unconscious. Unmercifully, perhaps, he lived. For surely living he would but crawl and see not, a useless mouth.

Then Derwent realized that Elgar and the others on the bartizan were staring at him. When he faced them, all turned their gaze away save Elgar, whose brown eyes, so like the Vicar's, were now like deep still pools, empty of expression. Derwent fled to his chamber.

V

The last rays of the sun caught the high cheek-bones and aquiline though delicate features of the Lady Edwina as her deep blue eyes appraised Derwent. A plain gray homespun habit that Derwent had not seen before covered her linen gown and her pale gold hair. Bare was her neck of the ilgras choker in the form of a great pard and rich with emeralds of the Eigin hoard. As she raised her long graceful fingers to his shoulders he could see that her fingers too were bare. In the passageway behind her stood gaunt Hacmon a head taller than the two grim warders who companied him.

When she turned to close Derwent's door, Hacmon moved forward as if to stay her. "My Lady, the Vicar bade me . . ." began Hacmon. She put his hand aside.

And now her voice came soft but with dominion

like a sword of finest steel. "I shall," she said, "do no hurt to myself here, nor to him. Not here, surely. By such honor as I still possess I pledge it to you. But I cannot say what I must say with you watching any more than I could do my toilet circled by kitchen karls."

"It may come to that, wench," said one of the warders as if to the other but loud enough for all to hear. When Hacmon turned to look on them their laughter choked and the blood went from their faces as if they were scalded. With enough of a bend to hint at a bow Hacmon shut Derwent's door. The hunger that had gnawed at Derwent through the day was gone of a sudden as he stared at his mother.

Now he could see that the fall he'd suffered was but an echo to her hurt. The disgrace of last night and this day were now made clear and hot in his memory.

He remembered that after seeing the bloody offal that once was Trajus brought in yesterday he had kept to his chamber through the long day. The defenders had loosed occasional arrows. Some Lothians set up protected viewposts round the fort, while others tightened the noose by piling kindling round the principal storehouses. The rest sprawled about or tended to the considerable body of horse they had in the north meadow. Derwent still had no longsword.

He woke late and did not go to dinner in the great hall at midday. He went to the bartizan overlooking the postern gate when he heard the herald's trumpet leading in a pair of messengers from Firnis, given free conduct through the Lothian lines. Alone now he watched the crowd in the common yard create a respectful circle within which the Vicar and his officers interviewed the messengers and examined the parchment, with the great seal of the King, that they brought from Firnis. But an hour later, the sun dipping down into the west, Derwent's hunger drove him to supper. He slipped late into the hall, keeping his eyes from others and gliding behind the arras to avoid folk 'til he got from the entry way to the high table. He saw that his mother's place was empty. Then he saw that his own seat, next to Elgar's at the bottom of the high table, was occupied by Hacmon's son Syljanus, of the same age as Elgar and long his crony. There was relief in the air as though the matter of the raid were settled and true it was that there was but a light guard upon the walls.

Derwent turned himself about and sought to leave the hall unseen. But as he went between one hanging and the next, he stumbled over a dog and lurched from behind the arras into the full light of the hall. As the dog had yelped, most eyes were on him as he popped into view, feeling faint, and holding to the arras for balance. "Look," cried Elgar, " 'tis a kinch in the curtain strings." And many folk fell alaughing, for true a kinch is a loop or catch in a rope but kinch also means a trick or sneak. "I call him Kinch," repeated Elgar, clapping his friend Syljanus on the back. And several folk laughed and pointed and called "Kinch, Kinch."

So he returned supperless to his chamber. And when he returned he found his mirror gone and his silver bracelet gone and all his clothing gone save his old all-days undyed homespun cloak.

All this ran through his mind. And now his mother, the Lady Edwina, stood stiff until the door closed behind her. The stiffness was more than dignity for now, with a flash of thigh, she brought forth from under her linen gown an object of the length of her arm covered with a gray cloth.

"I was given to Harold Holdering young," she said. "My line held the land west of Firnis when the present King's family were shepherds in the far reaches round Tordol. I was to give more strength to rude Southkirk. And now I and my family are nameless. And now lording it everywhere are the Lothian scum that were the butt of jests when I was a child in the royal hold at Firnis. And the upstart priests of the Eye mock us all." The Lady Edwina spoke to herself thus, her voice even-pitched and empty as if it were a child's repeating lessons.

"I was given to Harold Holdering young," she said once more, "and how can I blame him now who shared my bed for force of arms and now would shed me for the same?" And now it was before his eyes as if his mother, the Lady Edwina, had shaken herself awake. The effort was terrible as one who uses all her power to rip herself without a nightmare. She looked into his eyes.

"I am sorry, son," she said softly to him, "this talk will be so short and there is so much to be said.

Hacmon must have me on the road by sunset and I go forever to a convent outside Firnis to the north. Nameless as you, I am forbidden speech, and witch that they would have me, I am forbidden speech with the Vicar most of all. Do not think ill of him, son, for the message from Firnis was most clear. I am no longer Lady, or Edwina daughter of the Eigin, and you are no longer Master Derwent."

If the trunk is dead so is the branch, said the ancient law of descent. So I am Kinch, he thought. Holding the cloth-covered object in one hand she clasped his hands with the other. He felt as if life and warmth and determination flowed through her hand throughout his body. Kinch is better than Slops or Scut, as some of the kitchen karls were called. Kinch is a trick.

"I have three gifts," she said. Again the eerie dreaming tone was in her voice as she drew the cloth from what she held in her hand. His eyes were dazzled as the last rays of the sun were reflected as in a mirror. But it was not glass. It was steel. White with the slightest tinge of blue, the finest, most perfectly formed steel that he had ever seen. And it was not a mirror but a sword. Not a longsword such as man of the Kingdom or a Lothian might use, and use from the back of a horse. Yet the length of her arm from pommel to point and straight as the horizon on a waveless sea, it was no dagger or cutlass. Indeed, to Kinch's amazement, it looked to be stronger, sharper, and more wondrous beautiful than any longsword, any sword, he had ever seen.

"My father gave it me," she said, "when I put off my maiden priestess habit and came to Southkirk. My father told me it is a singing sword, one made by craftsmen in the south millennia ago, far before the Eigin dwelt in Firnis, even before the Southern Empire. There is no like one in the Salian Kingdom, or mayhap anywhere. The way to make such has long been lost. Perhaps lost are special charms, or the metal itself, or the way of smithing it, I do not know. Trajus heard of singing swords when he traveled far to the Southern Empire, but he said there were none there, just the legends of their making, a making that took three generations of master smithies smoothing the metal until, so it was said, the grain ran straight from tine to point, drawing the strength of the steel into the living strength of a sapling. . . ." Her eerie, dreaming voice stilled and she looked at the blade that she was holding with her right hand, and brought the point with her left hand toward her breast. Kinch felt a tingling shoot through his body and he reached as if to take the sword from her. But she drew back a pace and forestalled him.

"My father gave it as he had no male issue and my only brother was dead. He told me that I might give it the Vicar, or use it myself, in time of sorest need. Though I gave Harold Holdering my body I did not give him this, nor knows he aught of it. But now the need is sore. . . ." It now seemed to Kinch that she had returned from her dream. Her deep blue eyes surveyed the room and returned to look straight into Kinch's.

"I see, my son, that the jackals have taken your things. If not today, it would have been tomorrow, son. They have your blanket and I do not think they will let you sleep the night. Best that you not wait for them. They will not be kind, and you'd best avoid their sight or thought. There will be a place for you in the kitchen and I think it is in the Vicar's heart that after people have clean forgot the Eigin line you could be a garrison soldier." Kinch's face went hot with blood. A kitchen karl, he thought. By the Eye, a kitchen karl. He did not know the names of most of them. But he knew of their fleas and of the stench, and that they slept in piles together, cheek to crotch. Kinch was what they in the great hall had called him. A catch in a rope, a loop, a trick or sleight of hand. Kinch. His blood beat in his temples. His hand went for the pommel of the sword.

This time when she pulled back yet another step, the point touched her breast. Though the blade was laid near flat and came upon the surface of her gown as might the downiest feather, yet the cloth parted as the air before it and a single drop of blood stood there. "No," she said, and now her voice though not loud was truly terrifying in its authority and sharpness, "though the Eigin line is no more yet thou art Eigin. Though Master Derwent is no more, yet thou must be more Master and more Eigin than ere before." I am Kinch, he thought.

She looked down at his hand, which was inches from the sword's pommel. "And," she continued, "you shall not have this handle, for it is not worthy of the sword, nor of what you may become." The handle was fine leather strung round with golden wire, the pommel and tang crusted with jewels. He watched, frozen, as she laid the sword upon the table, plucked a small sharp knife from her gown, and sectioned the leather and the golden wire, stripping the handle and tang from the sword, leaving but the clean bare steel and the tine that had fitted into the handle. Though Kinch had winced when the knife first cut the handle, he now saw that its luster was more absolute without the handle.

She looked at the mess of leather and jewels and put them in her gown, muttering to herself, "May be it will buy my way undamaged to the convent where they'll immure me." And then she began to wrap crude rawhide tight round the tine to make a new handle, the sort of handle that a kitchen blade might bear. Kinch watched, the more amazed, as she sealed the new handle with glue and then smoothed glue over the lustrous blade and smeared crusted dirt from beneath the chamber pot into the glue. Kinch had the smell of horse renderings and worse in his nostrils.

She looked calmly into his stare. "If they took your blanket," she said, "how long before they took a singing sword? How long before they took anything but a house karl's midden poker?" And what she held out to him on her upraised palms did look like such, though his mind still held the lustrous image of the singing sword.

"This is all of the physical I have to give you, son," she said softly, and he felt her voice go through him like a spear. "And you must grow to be like it, son, scum on the outside and bright steel within—and perhaps brighter and better for your midden cloak."

He took the handle and felt the sticky stuff on his palm and smelt slop and rendered horse and yet he was content. Through his hand he felt a tingle, almost a hum, yet a hum inaudible to the untutored or undedicated ear, like the soundless sound of salt sea that a shell held to the ear recalls. We are Kinch together, he thought. And for the first time, though he still could hear their laughter in the great hall, the name sounded sweet within his mind and shameless. And he thought that though Kinch meant a snarl, a snagged loop in a cord, and hence a trick or sleight of hand, and also perhaps through Elgar's naming, himself, it had one other meaning. A noose.

And there had been two other gifts. But the sword was enough for now.

VI

Kinch lay shivering, his homespun cloak pulled round him, the carefully wrapped sword in the space formed by his back and the angle where the wall that held the storage cribs met the wall of the great roasting fireplace. Yet he was some dozen feet from the beginnings of the sprawl of bodies that slept huddling about that hearth.

Between him and the sprawl snored the great form of the butler, whose key and office assured him alone of a full measure of inner warmth. He was laid out over the hatch door to the buttery cellar. Butler was a pig-eyed, purple-faced choleric man. This was why Kinch lay shivering in this particular corner, the sweetish stench of Butler blending in his nose with the other stinks of the kitchen.

Butler was a kind of guard against the bully of

the kitchen, a scar-faced young man whose name was Bug.

Fortune had it that Kinch had left his chamber with the wrapped sword and homespun cloak to watch from the bottom of the stony stairs as Hacmon and the warders led his mother slowly across the common yard, past the great hall and the kitchen, and through the wide passageway that led between the gate keep and small inner stable out the main gate and to the road along the Ham, and may be thence, skirting the foothills of Rach Soturn and the Brineheld chain of mountains, north and west up the great southern road, through Moor End, Mirdol, and Mittol, and eventually past even Firnis where the King sat, to the isolated Anticore convent. He stood in a study, hearing the echoing hoofbeats that were but a whisper to the vast noise the Lothian horde had made departing but in the late afternoon sun. A cuff from Syljanus brought him to himself and he was grabbed by two young men.

"Hah!" said Syljanus, " 'Tis some kitchen scut." Then, pushing Kinch's chin up as if to discover who he was, "Yes, 'tis one called Kinch, and here we find this tricky scut, this Kinch, near the Lord's yard and the Lord's apartments, clear outside his proper place. Perhaps he's stolen something from his betters." And Syljanus patted his cloak and undergown. There was nothing but the sword and its wrapping.

Kinch did not struggle as Syljanus took and un-wrapped the sword. He knew what happened to karls who through clumsiness or momentary irritation resisted their betters. 'Til this moment he had held the common view that karls were oafs and natural cowards. Syljanus looked briefly at the discolored, rawhide-handled object, turning up his nose at the smell. "Ah," he said to the others, "this one carries his kitchen tools with him. 'Tis but a midden poker. And a foul beshitted one at that, apt to its bearer." And Syljanus bade them release him, handing Kinch back the sword and wrapping. "Take care you clean that well ere you bring it near the meat of proper folk."

And they left him then, for Elgar called down from above alaughing, "Leave that slime for now, Syljanus. Let us look to your new chamber."

When Kinch came into the great square kitchen chamber, some were already asleep, though there was still much noise from the feasting in the great hall. Many of the rest followed him with their eyes as one might follow an angel or flying devil, wings shorn and come to common earth. "Hast evil Eigin eyes. . . ." hissed a small child's voice, which was cuffed abruptly into a squeal and then silence. That was the last time Kinch heard the word Eigin.

His eyes held no fear for scar-faced Bug, who looked to be the only well-fed kitchen or house karl, indeed the only plump person in the kitchen aside from Butler, the chief stewart Duggin, Cook, and Cook's favorite, Maudie, who was in fact one of several cooks, though not named such. Perhaps Bug took no stock in the prophesies of the Eye and the more natural and ancient powers, perhaps it was mere dullness, for it was clearly muscle that gave him the weight that Butler, Duggin, and Cook had through the keys of their offices.

Bug walked up to Kinch as he stood just within the kitchen door, his eyes adjusting to the illumination provided by a few glowing embers in the great roasting fireplace. Bug poked him hard in the ribs.

Moving slowly, to give no appearance of hasty retreat, Kinch moved between two long work tables so that Bug could not follow straight away. When Bug caught up to him again, Kinch moved so that Bug's fist fell on the flat of the sword. And though the hardness of it was muffled by the wrapping and Kinch's cloak, and he was hitting to scare more than to hurt, Bug now stood, looking puzzled and rubbing his bruised knuckles.

"Here now," said Cook, "give it over, Bug, for the lad will be working 'fore the morrow's sun. Even the quality needs their sleep." And she laughed, crooked-faced, at Kinch, her mostly toothless mouth a huge black hole. "You do know that, Kinch, do ye not?" she said, and she held him close and he knew the odors of that huge black hole. "All work here," she said, "an' that for gruel and scraps." She took her hand from him then, and turned back to her sleeping place of pride nearest the center of the cooling hearth. Now Bug, stubborn in his authority, came forward once more. But Kinch chanced at this turn to have worked his way from the door past the cribs of the north wall across the whole kitchen to the buttery hatch, where Butler slumbered like a giant suet pudding.

Bug, closing on Kinch, chanced to step on Butler's apron, hitting Butler sideways with his ankle. Butler cursed and grabbed Bug's foot with one hammy hand and bit Bug's calf.

So Kinch came to be shivering, with the great form of the butler snoring between him and the sprawl of sleeping kitchen folk, his sword behind his back in the corner formed by the wall of the storage cribs and the great roasting pit wall, on the other side of which there still came a few sounds from the great hall. And Kinch laughed, though wryly and only within the secret chamber of his mind, and laughed for the first time since all began. Now Master Derwent is Kinch, he thought, and his sword of manhood a seeming karl's midden poker. His first fight a standoff with a kitchen bully named Bug. His first shield a sodden butler. And now his first campaign the conquest of a kitchen.

So sat General Kinch shivering and planning, his mind holding close for comfort the two important texts that his mother had set him, the one about her magic held closed within his mind for later rereading, the other, respecting Trajus, burning in his thought. For but three days ago a whole, seeing and striding man had said, "And to him," when his mother had asked Trajus to extend his oath. And somewhere without, perhaps at the garrison house end of the scum grounds where the overhang of the bartizan that overlooked the Ham provided some shelter, lay shivering a bloody hulk that had been that man. Most like he was not dead.

The horror of blinding and hamstringing was that it left a useless mouth, a helpless crawling thing that did not even have the eyes to catch the reluctant conscience of one-time comrades. Most times the thing would starve and sicken and die. But starve and sicken and die slow, with much time for regret and helplessness and shame, and hope and betrayal of hope. And his eyes had been so brightly blue and he had paced toward the signal peak with the solid easy grace of a blooded stallion.

From the great hall Kinch could hear the minstrel Kindrel sing that ballad that was called for by the last gentles when most were long abed, at that final stage of drinking when teary sentiment is more apt than laughter.

> As I was walking all alone,
> I heard two crows amaking a moan;
> The tane unto the t'other say,
> "Where shall we gang and dine today?"

> "In behind yon old fell dyke,
> I wot there lies a new-slain knight;
> And nobody kens that he lies there,
> But his hawk, his hound, and lady fair.

> "His hound is to the hunting gain,
> His hawk to fetch the wild-fowl hen,
> His lady's ta'en another mate,
> So we may make our dinner sweet.

"Ye'll sit on his white breast-bane,
And I'll pick out his bonny blue eyen;
With each lock o' his golden hair
We'll thick our nest when it grows bare.

"Many a one for him makes moan,
But none shall ken where he is gone;
O'er his white banes, when they are bare,
The wind shall blow for evermair."

VII

His mother's deep blue eyes had scalded him as he looked up at her first sentence since she had handed him the singing sword that tingled in his hand.

"My second gift," she said, "is a reprimand. You have failed your primal duty plain." And the steel in her voice softened but a hairsbreadth and that in her eyes not at all as she continued. " 'Tis true that the brunt of manhood comes early to you, son. But my father's father's father, Orthos Eigin, took the fortelesse Rerek deep in Lothia, and held it against two thousand Lothians for an hundred days with but eighty men. And Orthos Eigin had then but little more than your fourteen years."

And to his puzzled look she said, "These times teach men ill. You must set them right to earn your real name. But first correct yourself.

"Son, look you to Trajus: for he is your sworn

liege man. He is your all, your fort, your fields and
game forests, your mares, stallions, and foals, your
peasants and your horde, your bondmen and your
esquires, your warriors and your officers. For he is
your own by his swearing fealty and he is your only
folk. Look to Trajus, son, for you are his liege lord
and he is sore afflicted, and as I leave without
master save you." And Kinch's face was red with
shame and yet he knew more that his mother loved
him, but loved him as fierce pards or lions love, for
strength, not weakness, for bravery done and not for
long living.

With dawn next day Kinch began kitchen learning and kitchen labor with an art and a will that
even Cook marked. Like countless karls before him,
Kinch learned that kneading went well when one
imagined the dough to be one or another of one's
foes. He stirred and whipped, and scrubbed and
scraped, and mopped and fetched, till by the time
the great midday meal was in the gentles' bellies,
and the scraps and bread in the karls', Kinch's
untried hands had the beginnings of blisters.

"By that that sees, the lad's willing an' has the
art to learn quick, if 'e'll keep to it," said Cook to
Maudie as they took their midafternoon rest. She
might have been less happy had she known that
Kinch was slipping across the common yard looking
for Trajus with a slice of ham and a hunk of bread
under his apron. Theft of bread were no great offense but meat was not for karls, and still less for
castoffs.

Kinch however ate the ham and bread himself though his gorge rose for he was already full and the task that came with it was loathly, for aside from a few morsels all the fevered Trajus could take was water. Hidden under a low awning at the garrison house end of the scum grounds, Kinch wiped the dirt and blood and mucus and crawling things from those ghastly sockets, and smoothed clean rags filched from the kitchen over them. He cleaned and wrapped the bloody ankles and held for a time as a babe on his lap Trajus' great fevered head that had but two days ago hurled defiance at the Lothian host.

He is so much bigger and better muscled than I am, thought Kinch. He wanted to ask Trajus whether the skin on either side of the hamstring slashes needed to be trussed together with needle and thread. But Trajus was afevered and knew him not.

So leaving his cloak wrapped round him, Kinch slipped back unmissed to the kitchen in time for the first steps toward supper. Cloakless, he would need to sleep cheek to crotch that night. Yet when he came to sleep, sandwiched between the security of Butler and warm sprawl of his fellow karls, his mind was orderly. And he felt little of the shame and despair that had afflicted him yesterday, though his aquiline nose was still aware of the fulsome stench. Though Kinch did not mark it, his mother's second gift was to make him hale.

The singing sword itself lay below in the most secure place Kinch could think of for it in the whole of the fort, beneath some stones behind some unused racks, themselves behind the wine butts for next year's drinking, at the back of the farthest, most dusty, reaches of the buttery cellar. No place accessible to a trusted karl was more secret from casual inspection. The choleric, purple-faced, pig-eyed Butler, indeed, had long been disposed to allow no one to company him into the buttery cellar save for need on celebration feast days. And then he took only Scut, whose limbs were as strong as his mind was slow, and so most unlike to have the guile for pilferage. Albeit, and much to the startle of the kitchen folk, Butler gruffly ordered Kinch to company him to fetch wine for the evening supper.

Why it is that Butler chose this thing one cannot certain say. Most simple, perhaps it was that Kinch had chosen to sleep in Butler's corner his first night in the kitchen. Perhaps it was the still fillyish grace of Kinch, though Butler had some time back cast aside the body for the bottle. His mother's mother had worked in Eigin Castle and he had heard good tales of that as a boy. And true it was that Lady Edwina was perhaps the only gentle who had never once insulted him. She had but four moons back reproved a thoroughly besotted Elgar who had lit Butler's apron from behind with a taper awhile he served the high table. Perhaps it was that, isolated as he was from the other kitchen folk, he held in him some secret awe for gentles, even fallen ones. Perhaps it was the chance that the knee's ache came upon him and Kinch was nearest to his rheumy eyes.

Albeit it was not chance that Butler henceforth made use of Kinch in the buttery. Kinch was quick but free of breakage in following Butler's orders, and as days went on he proved an apt scholar for the lessons the strangely sweetened Butler found himself imparting about corkage and barrel maintenance, wort preparation, the judious use of resin, how to tell beer had finished greening or was near to souring, how to physic the common red wine of Tordol into a passable sack; and inevitably, and here Butler was strangely tactful, the more commonplace hall service lessons of food presentation, carving and sectioning at table, pitcher position and order of service, the management of the besotted gentles and late night wine watering.

Kinch woke early his second morning in the kitchen. Though cheek to crotch had kept him warm it had made him familiar with fleas. The kitchen was still. Even the laying of fire in the baking ovens was yet an hour away. The moon gave what light there was to the chamber. He rose and shook himself and felt the fleas upon him, doubtless feasting the more for his thin fair skin, and felt also the heavy glaze of kitchen smoke and the weight of the past days.

The common yard was quiet and empty save for a vivet who owl-eyed him and whinnied sweetly, the small animal's huge eyes catching the moon's near-full light. Trajus slept, and slept well, the ill heat in his forehead cooled. And somehow Kinch was suddenly without the walls, his legs moving with a

strong easy stride, as that a horse might set into to
eat up many miles. For there was sheer joy in his
muscles and in being private for the first time in
days.

He ran along the Ham through the dew-clean air,
the clean sweat slowly welling up beneath the grime,
as the rosy fingers of the dawn caressed the fens to
south and east and the great southern road, flashing
forward in the north to catch the upper reaches of
Rach Soturn Pikes. When he returned toward
Southkirk, warm and winded, sudden he felt the
pull of the unsullied water before the mill houses.
He threw off his apron and the kitchen gown that he
had trussed up to leave his legs free, and he leapt
into the cold clear water of the smooth rock-ringed
pool that nestled there. And that was good.

True it was that no more reason than a wild sense
of adventure sent Kinch in the pool. The folk of
Southkirk were not given to uncloseted bathing or
much bathing at all if truth be told. The gentles
were more familiar with perfume than water and the
common folk knew neither. But as he chafed and
slapped himself warm it came to Kinch that he was
most free of grime and fleas. And he resolved that he
would do this thing again.

He did not then know that he would come to this
each day as regular as cockcrow. Nor that he would
rise ever earlier for he would run ever farther and
swifter and with the grim will of Trajus companying
him. Nor that he would bathe thus even that week
in the new year when the sparkling snow held to the

earth at midday, though he was not then to tarry
overlong in the water.

That he was cleanly and stank not would serve
him well in the great hall, where he was to come as
Butler's man. At first, Elgar and Syljanus were to
jostle and pinch him, though not daring more under
the hard eyes of Hacmon and the Vicar. After a
time the gentles were to know him but as one who
stank not and was deft and tireless and unseen as
becomes the best of table karls.

And his success as Butler's man served Kinch
well, for Butler was to demand that he perforce be
free of the befouling and midden jobs which abounded
in the kitchen. Hence it was that Kinch had time for
his own affairs. Though, indeed, by the greening of
the new year all in the kitchen came to know Kinch
as one who worked hard and well when it was his
duty and went his own way when it was not. His
deep blue eyes taught them that.

Even within the first days Bug came to know that
somehow his muscle did not bite on Kinch, and
with that understanding came a sort of awe and for
the first time in his life a free obedience. Bug was
not to know that this cost Kinch the bruises of two
blows that he only seemed to avoid and the strain
his cheek muscles bore to keep his face empty of
pain. Kinch thought this was fair price for a man for
he who had nothing in his purse.

When Kinch came to Trajus again that day after
the great midday supper, Trajus was afevered once
more but he took both meat and bread from Kinch's

hand, though he knew him not. The great soldier's hulk that had fought an hundred fights and traveled three hundred leagues to the Southern Empire to study war prattled as if his mother succored him. But on the following day he spoke clear sense as Kinch fresh wrapped his ankles. "Amight have sewed it shut but the skin feels like to join itself." Both knew that severed hamstrings never rejoin, either in man or horse.

"Meat's good for healing," Trajus added when Kinch offered him what he had brought. Kinch spoke not.

"Well, man," continued Trajus, his gravelish voice as warm and wise as ever, "I ween Sorgun has had the Price for I hear no stir of weapon within the Fort here. We have given way to the damned Lothians too long. But I was over rash if athought to cast them down this time. Who'll put the choke-pear to the Lothians now must labor long in the field to bring all right to flowering. He must learn war anew and slow." There was a pause and Trajus chewed the last of the bread and reached for the water cup that Kinch then gave him.

"A man must think on the place of Southkirk," said Trajus, "for now 'tis the southeastern border of the Kingdom, the narrow entryport for Lothians, and we could stop them could we but hold the short stretch from the Fort here to Rach Soturn Pikes. They can send horse through the hills as little as through the sea water of the Cut. In all, but a mile or so needs blocking, and the Ham itself is a respectable wall for most of it. All boggy and treacherous for horse hereabouts. The best ford is some hundred yards wide and there be two or three other places where horse might force a crossing, save when the water runs deep in the spring and early summer. And the shallows change position with the whim of the river.

"Can't stop the Lothians with the force of horsemen that Southkirk can muster even if we stood ready at the ford to meet 'em."

And then Kinch saw with Trajus' eye. Though the middling prosperous port town of Southkirk supported round three thousand souls and might much more without the toll of war, the land abouts was not rich with grass for horse. Southkirk strained even to support the hundred horse and horsemen of its garrison. There were perhaps half that number in the town and nearabouts, and most for draft work, for aside from the great southern road itself and the road to it along the Ham there were but footpaths, and even the one that ran near straight as an arrow through the moors to Moor End was treacherous boggy enough to stop a single horseman let alone a troop. But even if one could sorcel draft bays into war horses that would mean less than two hundred horse to oppose least four times their number, and they the more experienced horsemen.

So one needed a wall of the sort that protected Southkirk's innards.

But the wall would have to move like a serpent for the ford itself and the lesser shallows shifted position. To build a fort on the ford were to try to catch the Lothian horsemen as man might seek to hold water in a sieve. How?

And Kinch had the eerie feeling that while Trajus knew not who he was, for Kinch had not spoken a word, Trajus knew what he thought. For Trajus said, " 'Tis a pretty conundrum, if we be not ancient sorcerers of power, how to make a moving wall. He that solves that conundrum, though he be but a karl, will truly be the Vicar of the kingdom if not the Vicar of Southkirk." But Kinch could not yet think of anything in what his mother had told him of ancient magic that could move walls. Still, there was that in Trajus' voice that made him unworried.

As Kinch rose and made ready to go, Trajus said, "As you be mute, you are a match for my blindness. Let us be companions together and I shall tell thee some of what I know and thank thee for thy meat and succoring." And Kinch remembered his mother's reprimand and thought that this liege man of his had waited overlong for his help. And Kinch thought of the ballad he had heard anights in which the knight's lady, hawk, and hound have deserted him and left him that the crows may pick out his blue eyes. Is a lord's responsibility to his liege man less than that of the man's lady, hawk, or hound? thought Kinch. And Kinch knew that he came to succor his man Trajus only as his mother shocked him to it and came two days tardy of his primal duty. And he

spoke not to Trajus for the sore shame that was in
him.

Albeit, he came to Trajus' side more frequently
and stayed longer, for such was Trajus' humor that
he spoke to Kinch of battle, of the preparations
thereof, of weapons and of the training of men, of
the statescraft that a prince must use in marshalling
them all. And perhaps because he had no eyes to be
caught by the present sad ruck of things, Trajus laid
all out orderly with maxims pointed and examples
stressed. So Kinch was schooled to war.

But it was not just his mind that was so schooled.
On the third day since his fever broke, Trajus
caught Kinch's sleeve and felt of his arm and then
of his apron and his thigh. "It is best," said Trajus,
"to look above all to the weapon that is thine own
body. Like to the finest sword it must be hammered
and cooled countless times, the hammering being
the making of muscle strength and durance. The
fighting men round here know naught of this, though
it leave them puffing in the brunt of battle." And
Kinch wondered if this man should somehow somewhat know of where he went at dawn.

"My mute companion," said Trajus, "you have
the harness of a kitchen karl but that is not your
quality. From the rude shouts that have called you
away, I gather that you go by the name Kinch in the
world now. But here in this corner we shall play of
times gone by or yet to come, an' ye be an Eigin
lord and I your liege man general." And Kinch

choked. "Trajus," he said, and his voice stumbled
high-pitched over the first of the name like he who
essays a troublesome or unused word, and then his
voice came full and rich and low with the rest of it.
"Trajus," he said, "how long have you known me?"

Trajus laughed well at that and said, " 'Tis an old
dog indeed that knows not his master. Though it is
daft in policy for me to call you Master Derwent,
Master, and still more for a time to breathe Eigin or
make the sign of the great pard—though there'll be
a time for that I trust. I knew your hands the
moment the fever began to cool. And I'll call you
Kinch for now save if you bid me nay."

That was a happy time. And there was a silence
between them, as comrades may pause first meeting
after a time, before they set on with the work.

And now Trajus squared his shoulders where he
lay half-sitting, coughed, and said, "You have my
report on the condition of Southkirk. For this season
there is naught to be done save to think what will be
done when you have power. And perhaps it were
best not even to think on it while nothing may be set
in motion. But we can now look to your own condition.
We'll plot how to build your wind and muscle, for
the smith who'd hammer out fine a good sword must
start with good iron. In a time we'll see to skill in
weaponry and the Armorer must see to you—but now,
certes, is hardly ripe for a display of warlike Eigin
talent." And they both laughed at that, and there was
a hearty grimness in the laugh. But it was not so long
before Kinch began his lessons in swordsmanship.

VIII

The new year was the Year of the Vivet, when on the winter solstice all folks gang about besotten and sing loud and dress in green and sometimes in full costume with goggling large eyes in honor of the northern vivet, the cat-sized but clawless animal that climbs trees and the like as might a man with hands on his feet, with amber eyes large as owls' and fine downy fur green as emeralds. In the first moon there was some cold that left snow at noon but winter in the main was moderate as ever in these oceanly climes, and with spring came the gush of water in the Ham from Rach Soturn and the Brineheld chain, and this with the sun brought the greenest year in a score of years, as most became the Year of the Vivet. And late in spring Bug put the young men of the kitchen to stave-fighting.

As staves are to weapons so stave-fighting is to

war. These staves were in length agreed with long-swords, and the mock fighting the karls did with them was an aping of the fighting warriors did with longswords.

Now the customed position for a warrior doing battle with such a sword is atop a war horse, and the length of the sword and the strokes done with it fit with this horsed condition. Swordstrokes are best delivered with the forward gallop of the horse adding to the warrior's arm swing. So we have the stroke-direct, where it is as if the horseman scythed a field of wheat, his sword swinging far out to his right. And the stroke-sinister, where the wheaten field is to the horseman's left, and the stroke is less broad, for the horseman's arm must reach across his chest. And the stroke-heavenly, where the stroke comes down from above. The parries that match these be the parry-direct, parry-sinister, and parry-heavenly. Those who speak of the stroke-nether, or the gorget-stroke, or the parry-all-besides, or any other, are but jackanapes or court-decadents, for the ponderous swift motion of the horse and the sword that fits with it allow only bold, full, manful strokes. Naught of the subtle or kinch in it.

This size of sword and manner of fighting translates strangely when folk play at aping it while afoot and swinging staves near their own length. Amidst hooting and laughter, the more joyous of the karls were given to running full tilt along the scum end of the common yard, atrailing a stave in the stroke-direct, looking as an ostrich might that runneth along swift but clumsy with one wing flung out straight, t'other folded up neat 'gainst its stomach.

That two karls, so set on from opposite ends of the yard, should come together with a proper stroke and parry-direct was less likely, as the Bug's matches proved, than that they fail to touch swords, or run head to head together, or fail wholly to come within any orbit of each other, whether through simple misdirection or slipping and falling. This was fortunate for those who fought Bug, for Bug likely began the game to further his simple lust for buffeting folk about.

Now Kinch was minded to join the game.

When he was Master Derwent he had used staves on two occasions somewhat so at the behest of the Armorer, who was a fully dedicated weaponsman and like to do what he could to breed a taste for proper instruction in youngster gentle or in warrior. But the Armorer did not have one running across the Lord's yard. Rather, one stood in place, or shifted but a yard or two suddenly back and forth, gravely swinging the wide passes of the stroke-direct and parry, the stroke-sinister and parry, and the stroke-heavenly and parry. But boys, and gentle boys, saw little in this rude sport where one might get bruised with such a stick as karls might use, and suffer the eye and wrathful voice of the Armorer. The warriors, too, were loath to undergo the Armorer's instruction. For they were daily employed in tax collection, and street keeping, in dredging and kedging, and seeing to quarrels amongst the fishermen of Inkling and the ship dockers and merchants anorth of the Cut. This made them indisposed to stave play that left purple bruises and had little dignity withal.

When Kinch told them of the Armorer's more stationary form of stave-fighting, Bug and the half-dozen stronger kitchen karls went hot to it, welcoming Kinch to the fray. Slops, an oxlike young man, was happy to have Kinch as opponent for while Kinch had gained the height of a warrior in the past half year, he was lean and his face still held a coltish grace. Slops did not know of Kinch's dawn runs, nor of the round of muscle-strengthening exercises that Trajus had set him.

So the four pairs did stroke and parry apace. Slops set on furiously at first, Kinch content to parry with his ponderous five-foot stave, schooling himself to waste no motion. Slops was panting by the time Kinch made his move. A rapid alternation of strokes-direct and strokes-sinister, a feint on the direct followed straight with a sinister gave him a solid hit. Kinch made his next hit a light one, for Slops fought on as one fearing blows.

In his next match Kinch was paired with Scut, who though dull-headed was strong and lively of movement. Here Kinch learned that battle is a se-ries of paired moves by the general and the oppo-nent in which moves the general must see the opponent's cast of thought and think one move beyond it to the doom of the opponent. And he learned that in this exercise one fails in thinking too well of the opponent as well as in thinking too ill. For Scut caught Kinch a sharp blow on his thigh when Kinch had made a finely executed feint which should have had Scut's stave in the parry-direct while Kinch's stave would be tapping his belly with a stroke-sinister. Scut had missed the feint entire, for he had charged forward, stave in front and eyes closed, as one who casts his fate to the winds. Kinch won the match by the simple pressure of a ceaseless series of strokes until Scut was fair winded and then Kinch lightly tapped him with what deftness a five-foot stave allows.

When Kinch parried Bug's first onslaught, he saw that Bug had made a natural and practical innovation. Bug held his stave with two hands, giving greater force and control to his strokes, albeit with some loss of reach. In normal battle or in the contests the Armorer directed, the free hand held a circular shield near a yard across. Then, particularly afoot, one could parry with the shield while thrusting under it. But without shields Bug's two-handed manner made good sense. And it was but Kinch's new supple strength and speed that saved him as Bug bore down on him with a furious series of two-handed strokes direct and sinister.

When the body be wholly engaged in a swift rhythm, some part of the mind may be made free to subtle intelligences. So it was with Kinch. There came to him a voice, a wordless reverberant voice bright as finest steel tapped lightly with a silver mallet. And the voice in his mind was the voice of that that laid wrapped in the back of the buttery, the singing sword of ancient power. And voice without words seemed to say *I am thy sword*.

Kinch shortened his grip on his stave so that it should be like that of his real sword. Perhaps some of it was Kinch's thought of that sword, but with his shortened grip he found he had more control and leverage with which to parry Bug's two-handed scythings. He found his stave forming a kind of shield in the air in front of him, a shield in the form of a door, though such a door as might be used by folk two feet in height. And this airy four-pointed structure easily blocked Bug's sweeping strokes.

Whether through simple inspiration or remembering how Scut had caught him, Kinch found himself, as he parried a stroke-direct, taking a huge step forward with his right foot, while at the same time straightening out his arm so that a line was formed from his extended right shoulder through the length of his arm and then his stave, a line that ended with a good thump as the tip of his stave met the pit at the bottom of Bug's breastbone.

Bug found himself breathless, sitting on the ground, simply confirmed in his awed opinion that not only fists but also staves did not bite on Kinch. This opinion respecting Kinch changed not a whit when Kinch helped him up and said thanks to the gods for a lucky stroke and complimented Bug for his energy and the closeness of the match. But somewhere in Bug, albeit he had no words for it, was the knowledge that Kinch, though garbed as a kitchen

karl, was a true gentle, a fair-faced and fair-haired,
fire-nostriled prince of Firnis, who would come some
day in a golden car to make all whole and proper in
sorry Southkirk.

Now perhaps at this point the karls would have
given up the game, for some were tired and some
were bruised, and the round of bouts had come to
seem to have somewhat of the taste of work about
them, and withal stave-fighting was no common
sight in Southkirk. But Kinch cheered them to it,
telling Bug to play more at it and not to hit so hard,
and encouraging Scut and Slops and the rest. So
they fell once more to it, for Kinch was minded to
test what he had learned of the point and the lunge,
of the tradeoff between length and swift movement,
and of the airy door-shaped shield. And he also felt
the exercise was good for him and for his fellow
karls, and mayhap there were lessons in it for all.

Kinch was light touching and made no point of
winning his matches as they played on. The bright
spring sun and the easy play of muscles were joy
enough. Indeed, when for a short space he took in
their play, the Armorer thought Kinch to be the
weakest of them for his leanness and youth, and
hence least likely to give damage or do some saucy
thing to his charge Syljanus. "Karl, you, there,"
said the gray gristly, leather-busked Armorer to
Kinch, "come here." And he waved the rest of them
away as Kinch walked across the common yard to
where the Armorer stood at the entrance to the
Lord's yard, where the gentles exercised themselves.

IX

Though the Armorer had given Kinch instruction some two years back, he recognized him now only as a lean youthful karl; a karl perhaps more cleanly and fairer visaged than most. The Armorer's need for Kinch arose from the distemper of Elgar, now undisputed only son of the Vicar, and the novel unwillingness of Syljanus to play shuttlecock once more to Elgar's mercurial changes of interest.

For Elgar had proclaimed that he was weary of the childish sport of stave-fighting. He bade his five gentle companions to join him in a foray to the Bear, the ale house that lay at the end of the docks in the direction of the signal peak, just past the temple of the priests of the Eye. And only Syljanus had said him nay, saying that he wished more instruction and more sport before he drank.

Now these gentles were not much given to stave-

fighting; nor was Syljanus. They found that the
Armorer's face had somewhat the color and raspish
skin of the pig-headed shark, and likened also to
the Armorer the loutish and joyless disposition of
that notable marine animal. And they would say
that that was not sport that barked shins. That was
not like to true battle that, with the Armorer about,
stank of priestly lessons and ritual postures.

But it chanced that this afternoon they had an
audience. From her not uncomfortable captivity in
the ladies' floor of the Lord's apartments, there
looked down on them a grave and fair-faced maiden
whose hair, dark as a raven's feather, coursed over
her simple cream-white silken gown to her waist.

Her ship had been thrown by stormy winds from
the south into a cup formed by the fennish coasts of
the southeast that led to Lothia, Tor Island to her
west, and the coast round Southkirk to her north.

Forced alee into the surf-clad rocks a league west
of the Cut but a week ago, all that now remained of
the ship after more stormy days was her floor and
futtock timbers and keel that lay in a snarl on the
rocks. What remained of her crew had set off southward on the great southern road, and Southkirk by
right ancient had salvage. Kinch and Butler had
four days past racked away some four score bottles
of wine from the Southern Empire. Cook wondered
over the doubtful herbs that had come to her in a
sandalwood chest, and the whole kitchen had been
put to kneading and baking, for the ship had carried
much wheaten flour and the sacks were wet.

And all in Southkirk had heard that they now held, mayhap for a rich hostage price, a maiden lady of the Southern Empire who was by some councils a princess and by others a high priestess. Those who thought her a princess or the like argued by her youth and bearing, and the richness of her wardrobe and furnishings that were already gilding the ladies and the chambers of Southkirk. Those who thought her a high priestess added that her green eyes cast evil about when the boatmen brought her through the town and that she had a savage jungle lynx for her sorcerous pet. This last was slander plain to the Lady Arlynn, for though she was in some manner a priestess, her eyes in the town had been frank and tearless as she sought to survey the place and manner of the folk who had made her captive. And the gray-green animal of the size of a wolfhound that lay chained in the dungeon cage below was not her pet.

Lady Arlynn had cast her green eyes on Elgar, Syljanus, and the other gentles through boredom and not through any lively interest in them or in stave-fighting. The simple boatmen and villainous warriors and country gentles who had hurried her here had taken her books. And they had taken the lyre that her father had given her on her eighth birthday some seven years ago, and that she played simple chords or scales upon when she would empty her mind for seeing. They had all her baggage save the gown she now wore, a sea cloak and buskins that she had worn for the storm, and two shifts and a purse that she had stuffed in her girdle when she understood that the boatmen and warriors who swarmed onto the wreck were more plunderers than rescuers. A boatman had prized off her ring. Indeed a warrior had shown a determined interest, whether avaricious or lustful she knew not, in her private person, though her eyes looked like daggers at him.

But the warrior was forestalled by an officer who brought her straight to the chamber in the ladies' floor where she had remained locked since. The officer gave testimony to a scribe while a grave, gaunt lord named Hacmon listened and made sure that all was recorded right and proper as concerned her maidenhood. A woman of the kitchen, a gray-haired duenna, and that officer came thrice a day to her room with food but they had no speech with her and were soon gone. So she watched often from her window into the Lord's yard and would have watched that afternoon had the yard been empty gravel, grass, and ivy, companied by the sound of the now gentle waves on the bar that crossed the Cut as it narrowed to meet the Ham under Southkirk Fort.

As it was she watched a half-dozen country gentles swinging staves at one another under the crabbed direction of the Armorer, and she heard the sea's music overlaid with hooting and panting and the clatter of wood striking wood. Uncompanied by the grave notes of her lyre, the thoughts that were in her mind were not seeings and were not good. Much against her will and that of her order, she had been sent for reasons politic to Lothia to be bride to a

Lord Sorgun. A Sorgun whom she knew not even to having seen his image, though she had had a rude missive from him.

Under the eye of the burly, gray-bearded Vicar, the ship's captain had told her that he would be on the road to Lothia's capital some ten days and that another moon would find her on her way to Sorgun. Bad it was that she had lost her prized furnishings and wardrobe. But worse yet that she was still upon her way to this Lord Sorgun, may be with a bridal price and shorn of a dowry. She could see nothing from her window. But within some few leagues of Southkirk were the Brineheld Mountains and somewhere there a mirror of water called High Tarn and a mountain called Rach Nord, and next those a retreat of seers if old tales held true.

Though her sea-green eyes looked over the six country gentles astruggle with staves, she marked them not. Now it chanced that Syljanus gave Elgar a sharp blow in his gut. Elgar, who like the rest thought her their earnest audience, choked back a curse at Syljanus. And now Elgar put on the laughing humor of a host who bids his guests move forward from the finish of an indifferent salad to a more sumptuous course, and all would go with him to the Bear. All save, most naturally, the Armorer, and also Syljanus, who said that he had not yet worked himself into a muck sweat and wished further exercise.

Elgar called to the Lady Arlynn as he left, " 'Tis a great shame, maid, that you come not to the Bear with us, for we leave but Syljanus and some scuttish karl to contest for your honor." And so Kinch was led by the Armorer into the Lord's yard and into the brooding green eyes of the Lady Arlynn, though she marked him no more than she marked the dust of the yard.

Kinch was aware of the eyes of the Armorer and of Syljanus and of the condition in which he found himself thrust. Though Syljanus did not condescend to address him, Kinch knew from his glance that Syljanus knew him. And withal this condition held peril for any karl. The Armorer said to him, "Now, karl, fear not. You are to cross staves with Master Syljanus here so that we may finish the day's instruction. Follow my commands and stroke and parry fair and you will suffer not."

But Kinch looked the Armorer clean in the eye and the Armorer saw that Kinch was no fool, and so, when he came to Kinch to put the shield on his left arm, the Armorer said in his ear, "Make your parries, lad, and he will tire of it in a space. He will not play the bully." And the Lady Arlynn heard these privy words.

So Kinch and Syljanus set on with round shields and wooden staves. Syljanus did a furious series of strokes direct and sinister, and Kinch was content to catch these on his shield, schooling himself to the rhythm of Syljanus' blows and to the graceful use of the shield. And when the Armorer bid him, Kinch stroked forward against Syljanus, but his strokes were measured and he made no use of the speed he had, nor of the greater control that his shortened grip gave him, nor of the lunge that he had discovered. So they battled on apace and neither touched the other's body with his stave. But Syljanus was puffing and his gown was dark with sweat and Kinch had changed not a whit in this exercise.

The Armorer knew from the first series of strokes and parries, and mayhap the Lady Arlynn soon after, that Kinch played as a gentle at Firnis or Imperium might play court tennis with his lady love, or his ancient uncle, or a respected fledgling of the King. So such a gentle would hit the ball each stroke into the middle portion of the back wall, and hit each time with the same measured stroke, and ever avoiding the corner shots, or the sudden change in pace, that trouble an opponent and make the opponent look the fool. Just as it is in court tennis, Kinch made Syljanus look a better stave-fighter than he had before, and in some small measure he made him a better fighter in truth, for folk learn well when all is set out slow and masterful and they not shamed in the exercise. And the Lady Arlynn joked to herself that in this rude country demi-kingdom, the karls were masterful and the gentles karlish.

Indeed, a part of Syljanus knew that though he might seem Kinch's equal to the passing glance, and a better fighter than before, Kinch was his patient master and the Lord's yard their school. But another part of him still ruled, and so he shouted,

"Watch now, milady," and after feinting a stroke-sinister, he leapt forward to the right, hoping thus to come under Kinch's guard. Kinch parried this by habit with ease but his eyes went up now for the first time to the window where she looked down on him, her grave and fair face framed by her raven hair that billowed before her over the window ledge, and their eyes touched and he was struck as one struck by lightning.

Now Syljanus caught Kinch a buffet on his thigh and said, "And now I have your measure, karl, and cease to play." And Kinch's face turned red with blood and Syljanus was abashed. Kinch laid on now with a blinding series of thrusts and parries, each ending with a light tap on Syljanus' torso, the last on the ribs that sheltered his heart. And in this action, though his face still held some red, Kinch was as a master carver who in instruction points with his carver to the suckling pig's vital joints but cuts not.

As chance had it, now came Elgar and his gentle fellows again. For the beer at the Bear had been sourish and withal the priests of the Eye next door were howling most villainously as might a cat in rut. And Elgar, who had seen that a pass ended with Kinch's stave atouch on Syljanus' heart but had seen no more, said, "Oh, what a sorry pass you have come to, scut-cuz Syljanus, that even a karl may kinch you a hit!" And his fellows laughed at his jesting manner with the words and at the shame that was Syljanus. But Kinch said quickly to Elgar, as one whose cap is in his hand, "No, my lord, it were no sauce on my side, for Master Syljanus and Armorer were having me learn the pass that Armorer taught Master Syljanus while my lord was gone." And Elgar was minded that Kinch spoke true, though it ruined his joke. For Elgar had seen that the touch was a dainty one, not such as one might give in a true match. And Kinch was a karl.

One jest in pieces, Elgar sought another, and as the crude craftsman, he used some pieces again. "This scut of a karl is kinch and so 'tis right we'll kinch him," said Elgar, and he gestured at his fellows that several took hold on Kinch. The Armorer coughed, and caught at Elgar's eye. But Elgar turned away.

"Syljanus," Elgar said, "you'll not gainsay that he tricked you that he might impudently tap your chest, so come you to our trick to him." Elgar led them off, four carrying the unstruggling Kinch and Syljanus coming behind, toward the low heavy oaken door that led down into the dungeon below the sea wall and the Lord's apartments.

The last at the door, Elgar waved up to the Lady Arlynn, "Shame that you were not with us for the beer, and now you will miss the meal, for we'll make the karl familiar with your cat."

The Lady Arlynn marked that the beer was said to have been sour, though true it was that this Elgar had drunk deep of it or the like, for his face had the color of a lobster that was boiled. She wondered whether the meal in the chambers below would prove sour or sweet. And the iron bradded oaken door shut behind Elgar.

Those that went before Elgar had stumbled on the eight stony steps but had caught themselves without dropping Kinch on the old straw-strewn musty-smelling rue-stained rough-hewn wooden flooring below. Soon they could see well enough, for the dungeon had several narrow windows that looked out on the sea finger that was the Cut, where the breakers sullenly sounded on the rocks below Southkirk Fortress. Two now only holding Kinch, Elgar, Syljanus, and the others all bent together to look through the broad but narrow spy hole into the cell that caged the gray-green animal that folk called the jungle lynx.

The cell was not the cage entire, for within it the feline animal that was like the size of a middling dog, a third the weight of a lean man and some lean three feet from muzzle to haunch, was held by a chain fixed by two links to her collar that circled round through two rings on either side of the cell, so that when the animal leapt toward the door as she now did, she could but come within a body's length of it.

They unbolted the door of the cell and swung it open and pushed Kinch within and bolted the door behind him, leaving Kinch and the gray-green cat whose hiss and pink inner mouth and gleaming teeth were but a few feet from him, and questing forefoot claws but inches. But both the jungle cat and Kinch soon knew that the cat could reach no closer, Kinch with his back gainst the corner of the wall that held the door and the cat at the limit of her circling chain. And Kinch saw that the jungle cat's eyes were lustrous pools of amber and her teeth gleamed whiter than the whitest ivory.

Those who watched through the spy hole at them soon felt balked of their pleasure. So Elgar pushed a stick through the spy hole and would nudge Kinch toward the snarling cat as one might bait an animal in the ring. But this, for the angle, could not succeed and so Elgar, with much cursing at Syljanus who would free Kinch, bade them unbolt the door. And Elgar would come through to push Kinch closer to the cat. But as he came through the low cell door, the cat lunged forward and broke the stud that held one end of the chain to her collar, and the cat ran at Elgar who leapt back, and the door shut an eye blink before the cat clawed into its inner surface. The bolt shot home. And when the more fearful were already upon the stairs, they all heard some noise in the yard behind them, and they rushed without, swinging the outer door of the dungeon aclang shut behind them.

X

The jungle cat did not move at once but stood at the door peering at Kinch with her large lustrous amber eyes, giving a cautionary hiss. Perhaps the cat did not grasp that she had free of the cell, for the chain was still attached to her collar by one stud, though the chain was now loose to run free through the rings. Kinch crouched in his corner, knees bent, his buttocks on his hamstrings, his hands up in front of him as one who was ready to fend off or to grapple. And they regarded one another for a time.

Kinch recalled that the jungle lynx was said to be a fierce marauder that thrice outwent the wildcat in size and ferocity both. Now Kinch was minded that unless his own apprehension or some trick of the sea light had increased the cat's seeming size, this fierce marauder were a full-sized jungle lynx indeed

for it looked a third part of a lean man in weight and
it was not fat-bellied, being some lean three feet
from haunch to muzzle. This largeness were further
strange because the sleek lean animal had paws out
of proportion large and she was a she, not a grizzled
pot-bellied tom. Nor did she play the fierce marauder for the nonce, for she but put her right paw
forward and batted at him as a cat might at a fly,
though perhaps more slowly.

And Kinch found it hard to do more than to
wonder at the sleek glory of the amber-eyed creature that was withal the moon to the sun of that
Lady Arlynn that had smote him so above. This was
her animal, or so folk said, and like to her in grave,
lean beauty. And many foolish stories went round
Southkirk. Some folk said that the jungle cat was
her familiar for sorcerous seeings, and some of
these thought that the cat assisted her in spell-
making, others that she could see through the cat's
eyes wherever the cat would go. Still others main-
tained she became the cat and the cat her, with
both maintaining size, so that in this exercise a
purring Lady Arlynn the size of a large doll would
be left in her quarters while outside would roam a
huge creature with the mind of Lady Arlynn and the
size of a lion or a great pard. Kinch tried to open
the book within himself wherein he had his mother's
third gift, what she had told him of seeing and art
magical, but there was no time for such a searching
in this scrape. Kinch shook himself from this
bemusement.

He would look at this jungle cat in the manner of Trajus.

She did not play the fierce marauder for the nonce, but she could do great damage to him with her claws and saber teeth. Kinch had seen a large tomcat kill a vivet once, his teeth grinding and strengthening his grip on the vivet's throat, while his rear claws ripped at its belly faster than Kinch's eye could follow. Kinch had never before seen a jungle cat, nor afore this had there been any in Southkirk and mayhap the Kingdom in living memory. So he resolved, having no other wisdom, to expect of this animal what he would expect of her smaller kin. And it is well that this council came to Kinch then. For then it was that the jungle cat's ears folded down and back along her head, and by that sign Kinch knew the jungle cat would leap forward at him, and she did. Things moved more quickly now than words.

It chanced well that Kinch was squatting in the corner, hands in front, for the jungle cat then must come on Kinch's hands that were palms outward as one who would grapple. And the cat might not sink her claws and teeth into Kinch's back, or legs, or buttocks, or any other likely part, but must first meet with his hands or ever she came at his face and breast.

Now this jungle cat, as any such wild cattish creature, could move more quickly than any man. But when she leapt forward, the whole weight of her body was set in a course to fly forward through the

few feet that separated her from Kinch, whereas
Kinch had to move his hands but quick inches to
catch at her collar and throat. Kinch caught the
jungle cat where throat and breast met with both his
hands as a man might catch a grain sack hurtling
down on him, and he had then the good sense to
push her off sharply ere she might claw up at his
hands and forearms. In the space of a heartbeat she
hissed and spat and lunged again, and again, and
yet again, each time Kinch fending her off, her
chain rattling behind as she leapt as rattles a snake.

After a time that was both an instant and an
eternity, it came to Kinch that he had fended off the
cat's lunge more than two score of times. He felt
like a juggler who has above far more bottles than
ever before, and who can by straining his every
faculty keep them circling in the air, but who tires
and begs for release and knows not how to bring the
bottles down without breakage. And Kinch could
hear his own panting as from a distance as yet ever
and again the jungle cat leapt at him and he fended
her off.

Then Kinch saw that the jungle cat's ears were no
longer folded back. And it came to him in a rush
that the jungle cat now was Kinch and he was now
Syljanus, for the jungle cat played with him as one
might gently instruct someone in court tennis, strok-
ing clean plays in simple rhythm that one's student
should learn well and not be shamed. With this
thought perhaps something in Kinch's manner
changed, for the jungle cat broke off her course of

instruction, and she ambled around the cell, settling atop the wooden bench that stood at the far
end of the cell under the narrow window. There she
stretched and scratched with her foreclaws in the
wood and yawned open a full company of grinders
and saber teeth and watched Kinch with her amber
eyes.

The angelus bell that presaged supper clanged.
The kitchen would not hold to account a karl commanded off by gentles. Nor would they hasten to
look for such a one. The Lord's apartments and the
yards above would be empty.

Now the jungle cat stretched, slid off the bench,
strolled a few feet toward Kinch, and then leapt
forward, resuming their fiercesome play of stroke
and parry. Kinch went to this exercise manfully.
And he was minded that the jungle cat now leapt
more slow and that was well as the light was less.
After a time went the jungle cat once more to her
bench, and all was scratch and yawn like before.
And at the end there was a simple friendly call,
more like a bark than a roar or a yowl.

But Kinch knew that there could be no fending
off in utter darkness. And he knew that he had
taken damage in their scuffling, for his hands
were astick and smeared with blood from glancing
scratches. And he wondered that he had felt no
pain, nor was in any way aware that he had taken
these hurts.

The oaken door above opened and closed again
most quietly and he heard soft footfalls upon the

stony stairs. Someone was at the spy hole though he knew not who for the outer chamber was dark. He stirred in his corner and brought his face more into the light from the narrow window. And he heard the voice of the Lady Arlynn for the first time.

"I had feared," said a voice that rang grave and clear and sweet as finest crystal, "that they would do some mischief to you, karl, when I saw them run back out and you not with them. Now with the dusk and your folk of Southkirk at supper, I am escaped from the chamber where they held me. I am minded to let you free, least you come to harm, but I must ask your bond, karl, that you make no alarm and do my bidding for this night and go to your kitchen and say nothing 'til the morrow." And Kinch heard in her voice the shame and scorn of one who finds herself friendless among country villains and that must ask a bond from one under duress and from a karl.

Before he might reply, the jungle cat, whose ears had perked at Lady Arlynn's voice, launched herself at him for a third series of stroke and parry, and for a score such passes and the like time in heartbeats, Kinch gave no speech. Then he said between pants, "As you see, my lady, your jungle lynx and I are making most bosomly acquaintance. The rapid progression of our intimacy has made me breathless and I fear unless you give me respite from your pet she will have all my blood. If you will unbolt me, I will gladly promise to do your bidding for the night and say nothing of you for a host of tomorrows."

She unbolted the door and Kinch slid across the yard of wall to it, his eyes on the amber eyes that followed him, and he was free in the warden's passage with the Lady Arlynn.

She looked at him and smiled and said, "Few jungle lynx reach near that size and they be sturdy males well on in years. If one of those had been in the cell with you, you would be hurt sore if not dead for they be marauders that outgo all cats in ferocity." And Kinch was minded of the large paws, and large lean frame, and of its kittenish manner and look.

She looked at him keenly and said, "I would not diminish your deed, for few have made companion of this animal and they only like you when it was but a kitten." And Kinch asked what animal she was and the Lady Arlynn said, "She is most lately weaned and has but a third of her full growth. She is a great pard. And she is not my pet but a most privy gift of recognition of Sorgun's lordship among the Lothians. Though with your folk here minded that she is an ordinary jungle lynx, he may never learn of her."

And in her last two sentences, the Lady Arlynn talked as to herself, and true it was that Kinch could little attend.

"The great pard?" said Kinch.

"The great pard is dun olive. The gray goes to brown or yellow, though the green stays save on the animal's belly and the inner side of the legs."

"The great pard," said Kinch, "that is the sign of
the Eigin line?"

"There be but one sort of great pard for aught I
know. In a book I had from my mother when I was
small there be stories of these northern countries,
and I read that an Orthos Eigin held a fortelesse
Rerek for an hundred days with a like number of
men gainst an hundred score of Lothians. Tell me,
karl, be there Eigins yet today?" Lady Arlynn was
amazed to discover that she was near to saying that
she hoped there were Eigins today, or any sort that
would vex the Lothians and their Lord Sorgun that
was so rudely eager for her. And she thought that if
she spoke so, she would soon be prating after the
place of the seers in the Brineheld Mountains and
the way thither. She drew her sea cloak about her.
She should not talk so freely and with one she had
just met and with one whose bond must not be
overburdened and with one that was a karl.

"The Eigin line," Kinch said, "is cast down this
last year. But folks say, my lady, that it will grow
forth once more as grows this great pard that is the
line's sign." And the vessels in Kinch's cheeks and
forehead were full of blood and he felt the beat of
the sea in his ears and his body felt aprick with
tiny needle points as one who is asneeze with an
ague.

The Lady Arlynn reminded him that he was her
bondsman for the night and bid him stay within the
dungeon 'til dusk was wholly gone and then return

to his quarters without giving word of her. He was minded to say more to her but she bid him nay. And he heard her buskins on the stony stairs and the dungeon door swung shut once more and she was gone.

XI

Though Kinch ran at an easy pace that ate up miles yet gave the tracker some look of the path, he could feel sweat on his face and torso that he had not felt in his dawn exercise, when he had run faster though less far afield. The day was the glorious blue of early summer that draws the eye unfathomably as if earth were inverted into an isle and the sky an oceany abyss into which one might fall endlessly. The sun that was near to noon still blazed on his back and shoulders from eastward. Eastward where he had left Syljanus and his horse bogged but a league out of Southkirk.

Kinch felt sharp joy that but a mile behind he had seen the press of a buskin in the path where the grass grew not, and one made recent and not by country clogs. Like the one he had seen in the dawn's light he had footed it flat. And Kinch joyed that she was so fleet and yet had left so little trace and crafty withal in her chosen path. For some three hours after dawn scores of horsemen streamed forth from Southkirk that would recapture the Lady Arlynn. But most raced along the Ham and then south on the great road to Lothia, and the rest divided the remaining roads and pathways on the off chance, and few were eager for the watery moors where horse went lame and where a lady would have no taste or reason to go.

When she had left him in the dungeon with his bond to stay 'til it be full night, he had gone to the spy hole to look in upon the great pard, for the last of the sun still glanced into the windows and he must stay some minutes to meet his bond. The great pard looked at him with her amber eyes and she barked at him, and soon he would venture what he had been forced to before, and he unbolted the cell door and went all wary but happy within.

But this time, though he took his accustomed position in the corner, she leapt not at him but paced slowly forward. And Kinch made his right hand into a large fist that her jaws would find it large to bite on, and she sniffed at his hand and her muzzle raised and her nostrils broadened as one who would fully know a scent. And he moved his hand as to stroke her but she shied back and went again to her bench.

Now came the dungeon door open again but no steps on the stairs. An unsure voice called, "Ho,

Kinch, be you there whole and still clapped up?" It was Syljanus.

"I be here," said Kinch.

"My will was to come sooner," said Syljanus, "but bar would not let me free."

Kinch came to the spy hole in the cell door and he saw that all that lighted the warden's passage was the taper that Syljanus had brought, and by that token he knew was night. Kinch slipped out the door, the amber eyes following him, and Kinch closed the door behind him and bolted it. And Syljanus was amazed. Kinch looked at him full in the face. And Syljanus said not what was in his mind but as one full startled and abashed he said what had been in his mind to talk of before he came upon this marvel. "When the others come not to the yard save the Armorer, might you show me the manner of those passes wherein you touched me at the end of our match?" Kinch looked steadily at him. And Syljanus said, "I have done badly, Derwent."

"Kinch is the name for this time," said Kinch, "and I shall gladly do more stave-fighting, Syljanus, when that we find a privy occasion." And Kinch led Syljanus up the stairs, shut the dungeon behind them, and left Syljanus standing in the Lord's yard.

When he went to the straw bed that he shared with Trajus next to the grain storage bin in the west wall of the kitchen, Kinch said nothing of the great pard or the Lady Arlynn. For his bond was given for silence 'til the morrow and moreover his mind was astalk with theories as to what all this meant. Trajus was weary and went straight to sleep with the promise that they would have proper conference in the morning.

Trajus had proved adroit at bean sortage, oyster opening, nut cracking, and the like, and he was fast approaching elder juridical status in the kitchen. Kinch had joked once with Trajus about that. But Trajus said, "One does with the materials at hand. Better a good karl than a bad lord." And Kinch had joked asking whether better a good karl than a bad king. And Trajus had said, "Lord, perhaps you need a pilgrimage that you may see a larger world and learn your fate."

Kinch did but one thing before dawn. He had gone to the buttery late for Butler and next him in the bed lay the singing sword, with a traveling cloak folded round it and secured neat with leather strings.

He lay then on the straw and opened wide the third gift of his mother, what she said to him of seeing and of magic in that grim dusk ere gaunt Hacmon and the warders led her off to nameless exile in the Anticore convent north of Firnis. For Kinch knew that the twin appearance of the great pard and the Lady Arlynn must call for some reply on his part and surely his heart was taken. And withal his mother had said that ere he reclaimed his name he must spend time in a place of seeing and learn himself, an ancient place of seeing, not a stall of the black-cloaked, mindlessly mumbling priests of the Eye.

"Son," she had said, her voice adream, her fair Eigin face and hair a silhouette in the dusk, "son, when I gave you the singing sword, I gave you plain the most solid work of crafty art and toolship that I could. And my second gift, the reprimand that I just rightly gave you, was plain with simple duty, and you will profit from my reprimand direct, for doing one's simple duty makes one better as a bowman and a poet are made better by the practice of their arts. So I have given you a material tool and put you in mind of a human one, but what are you to do with these? How if he who would be a bowman has no bow or knows no bowman to school him? And how if he who would be a bowman knows not whether he has a true bow or whether those who would scholar him are true bowmen and not dastards? How of the would-be poet who knows not whether his words be true words or if his instructors be true poets?" She paused and looked toward him and her face was dark, only the penumbra golden in the light.

"I cannot now teach you to see," she said, "and it a thing that you must do yourself. You must know yourself and, in knowing that, know the world and your destiny within it. And you must learn the great first lesson: that seeing is not seeing. This third gift you must find yourself." And she came more in the light.

"Son, you will need to go to a place of seeing. But 'til that time I'll tell you something simple of what the pedant calls grammarye and the vulgar

magic. There be four kinds and to all of them
applies a verse of the first lesson: magic is not
magical. One kind is the self-knowledge that you
will search for in a place of seeing. And that is a
way most hard, for you will lose your own self in it.
Another kind, a darker side of self, is the strengthening of the will within. Folk often use keepsakes or
dolls or symbols in this exercise of will and these
objects, though they have no power of their own,
may serve to strengthen the will. Yet a third kind
arises when priests use the fear of such objects and
other sorts of sleight of hand to make their victims
fearful or credulous or to work some other way with
them. And a final kind is the use of certain leaves,
flowers, mushrooms, and the like, that will relieve
illness or give endurance or vision or some other
weal or woe, and this most material kind is not like
to the others though the herbalist will often add
some chanting incantation or some smoky signs to
her dosage." And there was a noise without and
Hacmon called and she knew that she must go.

"One word," she said, "and goodbye. I do not
know which magic of these the priests of the Eye
employ though I know it is not the first. They hit the
inmost ring of the mark with some of their prophecies,
though often they be riddlewise about the more
distant future. And they are given to mumbo jumbo
and a poorly lot in all. I do not know what their
magic is but I do know it is evil."

And the noonday sun beat down upon Kinch's
head as he loped onward over the path that ran

straight through the watery moors, from Southkirk
up west and north the several leagues to Moor End,
where it would rejoin the great southern road. His
pace slowed.

Before him the path, for the second time in a
space of yards, was lightly pebbled clay clear across,
with no good way round through the watery peat that
pressed on either side. Yet the countryside had
lacked shrub or bracken that might hide even a
child for the mile since he had last seen her buskin
mark. Kinch knew that had she not wings she could
in no way have come this far. And Kinch turned
back upon his tracks as he was minded she had
done a mile before. For he remembered a thicket of
laurel bushes stood on a rise near the path back
some few hundred paces before that mark.

At council that morning Trajus had agreed that
Bug could make sure that the great pard was fed as
one would feed a growing lion. He advised that
Kinch should not simply slip away as might a peasant slip away into outlawry, or to sea, or to Lothia, or
to the maze of the city Firnis. Rather he must join
in the hunt for the Lady Arlynn in such wise as
might an humble karl.

"Then," said Trajus solidly and with no hint of
laughter in his gravelly voice, "you can privily ask
wisdom of this seer and help that she be safely
bestowed some place beyond the hand of Sorgun
and in that place perhaps also seek some understanding of your fate as your lady mother bid you.
And when you return some several days or weeks

hence we may give out some easy tale as that you
were taken by some brigands, mayhap the ones that
took off the lady, or some other likely account."

Kinch bid Trajus be free with his thoughts as to
what safety Kinch might provide the Lady Arlynn.
And Trajus chuckled and pursed his lips and said,
"Some hold it a prime duty of the prince that he
strive to prove irksome to his enemies and to those
who do great evil. Some truth to that, though not a
handsome truth. Should you keep the great pard
and the lady from Sorgun, you will hold from him
both signs and materials of his power. But a great
lord must rather be great in his loves than in his
hates. Your voice has told me of two such loves but
lately acquired and I met a third in our bed."

And they both laughed heartily at that. Kinch
held the singing sword upon his lap, still besmeared
and wrapped in coarse homespun, with straps set
that he might bear it comfortable upon his back.
Where the weight of the singing sword rested on his
thigh he felt a distant, muffled voice, and he felt
joy. As though he had eyes Trajus reached and
drew his fingers along the length of the sword.
There was a warmth and hush in Trajus' voice now
and Kinch knew well why many of the warriors, and
their officers too, had taken of past months to coming to listen at Trajus' side when he daily went to
the barracks end of the common yard after dinner
was done. And they came not to honor his past, for
they had but met him when Sorgun returned him

blind and hamstrung and cast down from captain general.

"Being without," said Trajus, "the sort of eyes that flank the nose I have in a manner made my fingers eyes. Certain they knew the sword when they came upon her in the night, however swaddled and begrimed. I felt the generations of ancient smithies and the song they drew out in countless forgings. 'Tis a most handsome blade, lord, and with your other new loves, she adds most sturdily to the Eigin House." And Kinch knew that Trajus let fall the privy words Eigin and lord because this was a leave-taking.

"Truly, does the sword sing?" asked Kinch. And Kinch had wondered late that night what portents there were in the coming of the great pard and of the Lady Arlynn. Now came the gristly sockets straight in his way and Trajus said softly, "And does the sun shine when I feel the warmth upon me in the yard? And would it shine should all below its beams be dead and feel not its warmth? I be no philosopher, Kinch. But even should we two be all that hear her song, yet she sings and it be a sweet song. And some day her melody will sour Lord Sorgun's hairy ears." Trajus paused to touch the sword once more and then his voice came again more softly still.

"My only wisdom is this. These three be not mirrors or clay that you can make of what you like and see nothing but your own face reflected therein. The sword and the pard and the lady have beauty and life and hard substance of their own, and by that token you must know that they are notable additions to your force and you to theirs."

Kinch saw the laurel bushes that were a richer green than the reeds and tough grasses and yellowish-brown surface of the peat. And his pace slowed and the pound of his heart quickened and he came to where the bushes clustered round like a wreath atop the small rise just a score of steps from the path. And he knew the Lady Arlynn rested therein.

The day was breathless still and the sun blazed in the endless blue and the thicket looked to Kinch as might a sweet water hole in a trackless desert. He saw some way within the laurel bushes the even-hued brown of her traveling cloak laid out over a maidenly form all modest and of a sudden he stayed to wonder in what manner he might fairly address her. So he came forward slow and entered the cooling thicket, and he was, for the sudden onset of shade, a moment blinded as he bent forward under the crowning leaves.

Their second meeting was thus to Kinch also like the thunderbolt, for of a sudden Kinch was thrown full forward that his face and breast and belly fell hard on the earth. And there was a body on his back holding him to that earth, and there was a blade close upon his throat held by a right hand while the other pulled firm at his hair that his head be held back and anglewise so the blade might keep secure converse with the principal veins of his neck.

"Do no rash thing, karl," she said him quietly in

the ear, her voice clear as a crystal wine glass, "for you have none of your folk close and I will cleave your life from you if I must."

And all was silence for the space of an hundred heartbeats save for their breathing. Then pressed on the Lady Arlynn saying, "I doubt not that you kept your bond, for one expects truth in karl as well as gentle, and withal you are but one person here or perilous far beyond your pack. But I must look to myself now and am alone. Tell me who comes behind you and how far."

"No one," said Kinch. He felt their thighs entwined, and he felt the press of her maiden bosom upon his shoulders, where the sword strapped round with a traveling cloak parted them not. "Syljanus and the other two stopped some two miles out of Southkirk and the rest are not likely to stumble up this way. 'Tis bad land for horses, though not for we two."

She slackened her hold upon his head and she said, her voice less sure, "So you be outcast on the road like I, poor karl, and belike because you kept your bond to me and that was forced." She shifted to sit upon the small of his back, so that she no longer rested upon his sword pack and shoulders, pressing him to earth as might a wrestler, though her blade was still familiar with the vessels of his throat. And Kinch stirred not a whit.

"I be not outcast, my lady," said Kinch, "at least I be not outcast as a karl, nor recently, nor in any way for the bond I freely gave you. I am on pilgrimage to a place of seeing and may be we shall share some stretch of the road." With her left hand the Lady Arlynn felt of his folded traveling cloak that held the singing sword, a hank of rope, a close-ground wheaten loaf and a husk-wrapped slab of hearth-dried and smoked meat, and a small pigskin with fire makings and a packet of Southkirk's whitest salt. She felt of the outline of the singing sword and eased some strapped folds aside that she might see some of the blade. And he heard the sound of her breath rush within her only to be let out after a time and slow.

"This is no karlish blade," she said. "I ween that it will dazzle sharp as the cut diamond if its smeary coat be off." She might have added that it bore the look of an age of forging and that of the finest smithies of Imperium. It had no rude country birth, she was minded, nor did this strange northern man she held to earth. And she thought what must this man be like should his karlish smeary coat be off, and she laughed at her thought and sheathed her knife and released him all happily and she looked upon his aquiline nose and deep blue eyes.

"There be," she said, "an ancient place of seeing high within the Brineheld Mountains where is a mirror of water called High Tarn and a mountain nearby that is Rach Nord. Know you of it?"

And his fingers led her eyes that she looked west and north to see some leagues distant the grim massy crags and screed valleys, flecked in the misty upper reaches by still-shadowed late season snow pockets, of Rach Soturn and Rach Soturn Pikes.

"Those," he said, "are but the southmost bastions of the Brineheld Mountains. Through them is the way to the high plateau girded by a score of mountains. And though I have waked each day to see the south of Rach Soturn and the Pikes glowering down at me, and have chanced to walk over the great southern road and into the foothills of Rach Soturn Pikes, I know naught of the rest of these mountains nor of the high plateau and its company. Nor will you find much better from the other folk of Southkirk. Though as ever respecting high places and the unknown, there be fearsome tales enough. I expect there is a Rach Nord somewhere up there. And shall we find it, my Lady Arlynn?"

She did a slight curtsy toward Rach Soturn as one who would say lead on, and she said, "Comrade, how shall I call thee for this season?" And he told her Kinch and she asked whether for this time it were Kinch alone and plain and he answered yes.

"Kinch for now," she said, her voice all crystal and abubble in his ear, "but like as not we'll find some additional titles on the way." And they looked full gravely into each other's eyes and clasped all hands together as do comrades determined upon an enterprise.

XII

The Lady Arlynn woke all at once from a dream of climbing, of the relentless testing of sinew and muscle, of footing, of handholds and of eye, as the twain won ever upward along the line where good rock met the scree and where the surest climbing was. The long sinews that bound ankle to calf and calf to thigh ached most abominably. But she knew from past days that this pain would cease once she had paced an hundred paces into the new day. And albeit her muscles were dead weary and fingers roughened by rock clasping, she knew that her strength was more than on their first day. That day when, having won their privy way through the watery moors across the grain of the moor paths and darkened to their thighs by the bog water, they came across the great southern road by cover of night. Then they picked their way when moon rose

across a ghostly boulder field and onward what
Kinch counted a safe distance through blue-black
seeming bracken into the western foothills of Rach
Soturn Pikes. So over three days Kinch had forced
the pace round west along the Pike and then eastward up the great ridge that joined it with Rach
Soturn. And then along that ridge and onto the
eastern face of Rach Soturn that was awesome grim
and steep to behold from afar but of honest rock and
fair for to climb, and they on the rope but thrice.

Through those days the mountain embraced them
as a lover might with its panoply of solemn and
joyous beauties. As when the dawn sun smote the
highest crags and gently fingered the purples and
greens of the misty, dew-sparkled lower valleys.
As when the noonday sun backed the upper ridges
and all was still and silent save when an emerald-
green hummingbird came to greet them and would
in all that vastness look only to the Lady Arlynn's
red kerchief for nectar. Or as when late in the day
they paused and heard the occasional thunderings
as the last rays of the sun would send one more icy
pocket acrashing. And then they looked over tiny
Southkirk and the moors into the vastness of the sea
that shaded from gray-green to wine-blue as it reached
toward Tor Island that brooded shadowy and mysterious on the horizon some ten oceany leagues to the
west and south. And she had no plaint that the pace
was harsh, for she knew that Kinch's dried meat,
however stringsome and endless to chew, would last
but a few days more and the mountain blueberries

and lime-green gorse berries were sour and insubstantial fare and they but now reaching the beginnings of the high plateau.

Now full awake, she knew that it was but an hour of dawn. She looked from the blackness that folded round her cloak and leafy bower and from the soft gray light of the last of the full moon that shone in the cave's mouth near Kinch's bushy nest. And she heard a voice whisper, a body's length from her ear around this black end of the cave's long lip, "He is alone. And but one can leap in on him in that hole. We'll have the kid make the slaughter of him, for he sleeps deep upon his belly."

The Lady Arlynn's knife was in her hand and she all silent like a pard came through the blackness to where Kinch lay, and the youth that then leapt upon his back failed in the first stroke of his cutlass for it caught on rock as he swung it down, and that burly youth had no second stroke for she was on him and had pulled her knife across his throat, digging in for the two great veins and cleaving back even to his neck bones ere ever he knew he had to do with another.

She leapt back from him to win free from a last stroke at her and she saw his blood spill black in the moonlight down his breast as he stumbled at her and she saw his eyes mazed and then empty. Behind him rose up Kinch full naked with the singing sword in his hand.

Kinch leapt through the mouth of the cave and some paces to the right ere the four that remained

were ware of him. For Trajus had said that the
warrior who enters a chamber of foes must bolt
quickly through the entry way and to a side and
Kinch thought that the cut they stood within was but
a large chamber, and his choice of the right chanced
well for he now barred their way outside the cut.
The nearest brigand came at Kinch with an iron
shortsword. Kinch gave him the stroke-heavenly and
his sword shattered before that stroke as shale before a sledge, and the singing sword sliced on through
leather, skin, and muscle 'til it bit his house bones.
Kinch kicked him aside as the second man ran at
him.

This second brigand had lost his wits for he ran
at Kinch with a small dagger held low and no guard.
Kinch swung a full two-handed stroke-sinister that
left the man's head most parted from his body, and
the wreckage left pulsing jets of blood like a hog
hung from the rafters for the slaughter cut. Kinch's
face and breast were spattered with blood and his
gorge rose. But he knew there were no treaties with
these fierce mountain robbers. If now let by, they
would follow their trail and bring their fellows to it
like wild dogs.

The last two set on against him together, but their
weapons were but brass cutlasses like to slit a sleeping throat or frighten a merchant and in no way apt
to the hot gates of battle. Kinch's first stroke, glancing upward off the brass, made a gruesome hodge-
podge of one man's throat and jaw and teeth, and
Kinch lunged through the final man's flimsy guard

to bury the singing sword near to the hilt in his chest. And pulling forth his sword Kinch gave the death blow to the first man he'd faced, that had striven upward, his shattered sword still in his hand.

Now Kinch stood atremble, his breath coming in labored shallow gasps as one who strives not to fall vomiting. On him shone the last of the moon and the faintest beginnings of the sun, whose rise was presaged by the faintest roaring in the air that came ever before dawn in these mountain reaches. His sword arm and hand and the handle it gripped were so splashed with blood that they dripped ever and anon onto the rock and onto his feet, and the sparse blond hairs of his chest were matted with blood; and here and there the rest of his body and principally his face and shoulders were splattered and smeared with blood that in that light looked more like black bog water clotted thick with dust. And the Lady Arlynn took the bloody singing sword from his hand and took his bloody hands and led him nearby where was a small spring, and all gently she washed the clinging blood from his face and arms and hands and shoulders and chest, and she washed where the obel-sized freckle sat above his right buttock like a rock thrown on a field of snow and onto his ankles and feet that were adrab and aclot with blood. Then she took the singing sword, whose grimy midden coat was now soaped with blood, and she washed the sword clean and wiped all clean with her red kerchief and in the blaze of the new dawn the singing sword shone like a second sun.

And they were late on their path that morning, for hard it was to find ground for burial and to dig five shallow holes. But they would not leave a banquet for the ravens of the mountain.

XIII

"This morning," said Nim, "you will run three times round the lake. Let your mind empty of all but the movements of your strings and muscles and of your heartbeats and of your breath. And you will find me here when you have done."

Master Nim grinned at Kinch like an ancient monkey from where he sat, gnarled legs and well-callused feet folded all neat beneath him. His back rested lightly on a pine whose roots stretched far and thickly that it held itself in the thin soil next the lake on that high wind-swept plateau, the lone tree midst the blue-green lichen and the emerald and olive mosses and the sparse speary cat grasses that fringed the lake, but a tree whose thick gnarly trunk quickly narrowed to a small sapling no higher than a man might stand. And mayhap the Master Nim was like unto that tree, for what he taught was clean, simple, beautiful, small, and true, but albeit so plain that it was rooted thick and crafty into the bone of the earth that it might not be conjured away by the most windy prophet or artful mage.

The Lady Arlynn and Kinch had come to the place of seeing toward the end of their second day on the high plateau. Several small buildings huddled under the lip of a western ridge, their walls unpainted mountain pine, smoothed and silver-grayed by the bright sun, clear rain, and unsullied wind of these high places, and next them, to south and east from whence the twain pilgrims came, the cold shimmering pale-blue waters of High Tarn in whose midst stood alone an ancient stony high-arched gate, while brooded over all the tumbled masses of Rach Nord, whose sheltered glacier ever fed High Tarn. There came the clear clang of a small bell as they approached, and near all the folk of that place came forth to watch the sunset that sped through its ruddy rainbow into darkness in these high reaches and to watch the rise of pale-green Demeter in the purpling east.

In their simple travel cloaks, the Lady Arlynn and Kinch blended well with the masters, students, and most of the guests, who wore plain undyed homespun robes. And they were welcomed into the supper meal of wheaten bread and herb and bean soup. And afterwards the ancient seer woman Gro interviewed them and then led them with a small lantern through the starry dark, Arlynn to a senior student cell and Kinch to a guest bed; for though he

was given to Nim for instruction, his stay would not
be long and he would not study the special lores
here fostered such as astronomy, epic poetry, mountain flowers and mosses, and the history of Salia
and Lothia.

Gro assured Kinch with much toothless grinning
that his course of instruction with Master Nim might
well be short, for all he had to learn was that seeing
was not seeing and that in short the Master Nim had
nothing to teach him. Kinch asked Gro why he
should go at all to Master Nim if Nim could teach
him nothing. And Gro said, "To learn nothing may
be done quickly but it is a learning that all within
you will resist and you must lose your soul in
gaining it." And Kinch asked whether he would
learn his fate and she assured him that he would
and Kinch was puzzled by the old woman's words.

When Kinch had finished his three circuits of the
lake, he came once more before Nim, who still sat
with his back against the tree. And Nim stated in
short Kinch's account of himself, that he would
know what was his fate and of the forces with which
he would have to do, and that his mother, somewhat
a seer and now put by through circumstance, had
laid it upon him that he should go to a place of
seeing and learn of its inmost wisdom. Nim's account had but little less of particulars than Kinch's
own, for Kinch had breathed no word of Eigin, or
Vicar Harold Holdering, or the Lady Edwina.

"Were I," said Nim, "the great god that weaves
men's fates or some godlet that assisted that god,

mayhap I could tell you that the Lord Sorgun would
do murther on you this winter solstice. How would it
serve you to know that this was your fate?"

"Why then," said Kinch stoutly, "I would take
caution to evade his blade."

"If," said Nim, "I were the great god and your
fate was to be so murthered, you would be murthered
so whatever your cautions. And if your evasion
succeeded then by that token you would know that
I was not the great god and that it was not your fate
so to be murthered." And Nim smiled faintly as one
who shows a child once more a simple sum. "So it
serves not the seer to know his fate. Seeing is not
seeing. And be there such great gods, they know
this well, for the great gods are silent."

"But why then are there fortune tellers in Southkirk's market, and why do folk worry whether the
moon was in a certain octrand when they were
born?"

"Hah!" said Nim, clapping his hands together,
"when the huckermuckery of fate and the great gods
be spoke of, the vicious murky end of the market
cannot be far behind. As when a sooty prophet of
the cards will tell some moon-faced youth that there
is a great love somewhere in his future and the
youth will then fall with rude assurance on whatever
maid or drab chance puts in his path. As when that
sooty prophet will most murkily hint to the tremble-
faced merchant of some reversal and of a charm that
may ward it off, and if fly fortune right, the merchant will applaud the charm, and if fortune is

sinister, the merchant will applaud the prophecy, and all ways the prophet of the cards will prosper. When folk go to such prophets, they but wish a shadowy mirror of their fears and wants, a self-portrait with some touch of gilt and high drama and no wens or pox marks or hairy freckles." And Master Nim held out his empty hands and was silent. And Kinch was minded of Trajus' praise of the singing sword and the great pard and the Lady Arlynn, that they were not mirrors or clay for his designs but with a texture and a force of their own.

"What of the priests of the Eye?" asked Kinch.

And Nim was silent to this question and flared the nostrils of his lean nose that was bent like an eagle's beak and Nim looked narrowly at him and it seemed to Kinch that a quietness had come into the thin cool air as if the mountain listened.

"Yes," said Nim finally, "they are a little mystery for sometimes they seem more than market soothsayers, and we will talk to them anon, after these lessons, for the Eye has little to do with not seeing." And Nim shook his head and then grinned as someone who returns to a familiar path. "You will now run five times around the lake. Let your mind be empty of all but the movements of your strings and muscles and of your heartbeats and of your breath. You will find me here when you have done."

While they climbed Rach Soturn, Kinch had asked the Lady Arlynn how one was schooled to understand that seeing was not seeing. She had told him that he must simply do what his master said and not think on what might lie behind it, and that the lessons might take days or months, and that the lessons were not that he should learn one thing or another but that he should learn not to see and that the master would understand that he had learned to not see when he gave a worthy answer to a question his master would put him. And Kinch reflected that it was well he was inured to running for otherwise he would have by now a surfeit of it. But as he turned to go Master Nim spoke again, pointing toward the ancient stony high-arched gate that stood, moss-greened in its lower reaches and bare stone above, in the middle of High Tarn.

"Countless centuries ago," said Nim, "that gate was raised by the Master Buridan. It is built as one might build a gate in the walls that folk might come from the outer country inside a city, or as one might build the main portal of a great house through which folk might pass from the outside world to the inside one. But Master Buridan built no walls, nor any house, but just this stony arch, so that one would be hard put to say which side was inside and which outside. And the Master Buridan called it the Gate of Enlightenment through which one might pass from ignorance to the secret behind all worlds.

"And the question that I put to you, Kinch, is this. Which side of Buridan's gate there is the inside, and which the outside, and how may the wayfarer pass through the gate to enlightenment?"

Kinch stared at the stony arch and wondered at

Nim's challenge, for Kinch was minded that were
the gate built so, there could be no foundation for
saying, of one side, that it was the inside and the
other the outside. And Kinch was of a mind that
perhaps this conundrum was but a tricky net of
words in which he might flail about forever. And he
wondered whether this was the same true of Trajus'
conundrum about a wall that might move athwart
the Ham and so hold the Lothians from the innards
of the Salian Kingdom.

Kinch ran and ran endlessly, his mind empty of
all but the voiceless rhythm of his muscles, strings,
and bones, and the feel of the scabby lichens and
hairy mosses and bony rock beneath his bare feet,
and the warm cascade of the sun through inconstant
misty clouds that ever and anon bared and embraced the surrounding mountains, and the ever
changing windlets that cooled him from one direction and then another.

And when he came to the end of the rounds that
Nim had set him, Kinch was minded that he had
attained that state in which seeing is not seeing,
even that state that Nim had spoke of when Kinch
showed him the singing sword.

For on that first night when Lady Arlynn and
Kinch had come to those watching the final light of
day, Master Nim, whom Kinch then only knew as
an old man among those who greeted them, had
reached for the bundle that Kinch carried on his
back and asked that Kinch show him his sword.
And Kinch had drawn forth the singing sword that

blood had soaped clean and the old man's eyes had gone full wide and his gnarly fingers had trembled as he gently touched the blade, and gesturing the others by as one who had authority, he said that he would see the sword move. And Kinch, as one who would please his host, swung the blade this way and that.

At this the old man put up his hand and said that he had asked that the sword move, not that Kinch swing the blade this way and that. And the old man said that one day he would see this sword and Kinch move as one, neither swinging the other. The old woman Gro bid all go in to supper. Kinch passed near the old man that he was to know on the morrow as Master Nim and Kinch saw that the old man's cheeks were streaked with tear tracks. And Kinch wondered how a sword might move without a man swinging that sword and he wondered that the old man should have both tears and joy at once and over such a thing. Later that night, after Gro had conducted the Lady Arlynn to her cell and Kinch to his, Kinch wondered whether the singing sword had pared the life from the four brigands of Rach Soturn, for he saw in memory that he had not swung the singing sword, but that all from first to last had simply happened without more of his ado than as grass might grow or rain fall.

Well it was that Kinch was inured to running, for as the days went by, the Master Nim would talk less and less and he would ask that Kinch sit looking at this or that rock or stem or other small thing, and ask ever and anon that Kinch run such and so a number of times round the lake. And Kinch knew that he was not to think in this exercise but ever to know that even as there was no difference between his mind and his body, so there was no difference between his and not his but both moved together and were one, and Kinch was minded that Master Nim chose the number of rounds that Kinch would run by throwing dice within his head, which is to say by chance.

Kinch asked the Master Nim how he picked these numbers and whether what he was minded was so.

And in answer the Master Nim drew Kinch's eye close to a tiny branch of the gnarled pine tree gainst which it was Nim's wont to rest his back. Kinch saw that three ants were busily moving upon this twig, and as he watched one ant left the twig, perhaps bearing a bit of sap to an ant haven below the tree, and then two more replaced that one, and Kinch watched as the number of ants upon that twig ever waxed and waned.

"Look you there," said the Master Nim to Kinch, "and see that these ants do not play at dice, for each goes about his duty, some searching for sap and tinier creatures and other things needful, while other brethren bear such back to their common home. And by this you will know that the number I set you each time was not produced by a dice box or my idle thought, nor is it some geometer's learned series or a mystic's number such as the number of fingers held up in sequence by the monsters extramundane in the great frieze at the main portal in the Emperor's place in Imperium, nor is it the number of days in your life or any other matter of yours. 'Tis but simple nature, right orderly and full of purpose, but concerned with you not a whit."

"So," said Kinch, "you simply counted the number of ants upon this twig and told me to run this many times around High Tarn?"

"Even so," said Nim most gravely, "though I will own that yesterday morning a sizable beetle sat upon that twig and over a score of ants postured themselves to do battle with it, and I had no heart to call out to you a like number. One can take only so much instruction from indifferent nature." And here Nim smiled a smile most sweet and simple and he and Kinch fell alaughing heartily.

Kinch rose then and stretched and felt the salty sweat that was upon his skin and he put off his undyed homespun gown and dove into the shimmering pale-blue waters of High Tarn. And those waters closed as an icy pure girdle round him and his breath blew from his lips, but after a space it came again in great gasps and he set forth apace most strongly, cupped hand over cupped hand and his feet ever abeat behind in muscle-warming strokes, toward the rocky arch that stood alone in the center of that lake. And as he swam Kinch heard in his mind those words that Master Nim had said about gods.

"The first great god," had said Nim, "that one hears of is said to have spumed forth his milky seed from heaven upon this earth. Thus have we rain and the spreading fruitful ruck of living things and we the great god's fondest progeny. What a reading-in of human form and human rut into the indifferent fabric of the world! Might not the beauteous run of creatures and the sparkling rain rise up in offense that we make nothing of them but a mirror of our sweaty dreams? No, Kinch, forgo these great gods that you can do justice to these little ones as this ant, or that blade of grass, or the hummingbird that came to the Lady Arlynn's kerchief, or you and I."

Kinch swam by the moss-haired stones and through that high-arched gate and then swam back to where the Master Nim stood watching him. And burning in Kinch's brain were those words of the conundrum that the Master Nim had set him, "Which side of Buridan's gate is the inside, and which the outside, and how may the wayfarer pass through the gate to enlightenment?"

When he came ashore, Kinch saw that Nim was staring at the obel-sized brown mark that stood above his right buttock, like a brown rock thrown on a field of snow. But he stoutly said to Nim, "I can now tell you, Master Nim, which side of Buridan's gate is the inside, and which the outside." And Master Nim signed that he should say his piece.

"A city or house," said Kinch, "is much like a bottle, and a gate, a bottle's lip." And he thought fleetingly of purple-faced Butler, and the buttery wine racks, and the glass blower's house in Southkirk.

"If we," Kinch went on, "draw a line across the

lip of a bottle, one side, at most a lungful of wind, is of points that are inside the bottle. And all the points on the other side—in brief the rest of the world entire—are outside.

"But now suppose we blow within the bottle that it grows ever larger and larger and larger so that the inside gradually fills up the world 'til there be no room left for the outside, and of any point in the world it becomes both inside and outside, for when one passes through this lip or gate one ever comes into one and the same world. So as I read Master Buridan's puzzle, whichever way I swim I am enlightened to learn that I am in the same world. It is only I that am changed." And Kinch stopped and panted as one who has run apace and truly he felt suddenly cold and he put on his gown.

And the Master Nim looked at him with a grin and clapped together his hands and he said, "There are less strenuous ways to reach enlightenment, Kinch, but I judge you have answered Master Buridan." And then, to Kinch's amazed eyes, Master Nim threw off his monkish habit and leapt into those cold pale-blue waters of High Tarn that shimmered in the sun. And Kinch feared that the old man's heart would burst with the work upon his muscles in swimming and the warding off of cold, but Nim swam off solidly and passed under Buridan's gate and swam back to where Kinch waited him upon the shore. And when the Master Nim came then ashore, looking somewhat as might a bluish monkey for the cold though he said *hah* and *ho* most stoutly, Kinch chafed his ancient flanks that he might be warm, and then did Kinch stand stock still for he saw an obel-sized brown spot on Master Nim's back just above his right buttock, like a brown rock thrown on a field of snow.

And the Master Nim rapidly put on his habit, looking through Kinch's puzzlement as might a man look through ten leagues of empty air, and walked briskly off.

XIV

That afternoon the Lady Arlynn and Kinch paced toward its glacial source in Rach Nord one of the rivulets that succored High Tarn, a silver braid that gurgled sweetly over the rocks and bubbled through the emerald mosses and sparkled and shimmered in the brazen sun.

After a time they were of a height that they might see the houses of the place of seeing as a child's playing blocks cast down near a garden pond with a tiny pebbly arch through which golden fish might swim. From where they stood, they could see the slender path that led from the houses along the lip of the western ridge and then disappeared from view as it went down toward the west and thence toward Firnis. And they could see most of the high plateau that faded some leagues south into wispy mist, pierced some miles farther by the highmost crags of Rach

Soturn. A gray sea eagle screamed in the distance above them as it soared upon a windy wave that bore it southward. And was a small shielded glen there, held like a cup that drank the westward sun and whose warm flat rocks were pillowed here and there by dry moss and tiny white dewcup flowers.

Their eyes drank deep on one another and all gravely she brought up her arms that her slender fingers might cup, frame, and touch of his face. His hands were atremble that grasped the Lady Arlynn close, breast against breast, that they might be still. And her breath came forth in a little cry that was half a laugh and half a purr, and their lips were firm fused and as with the rest of their hot coming together one could not say which was the hammer and which the anvil but that the fire was white and the metal gold incorruptible and the work of hearts compact. She said, *I must see*, and pulled his habit from him and saw, even to his Eigin birthmark and bullish particulars. And the sun was glorious bright within that glen and all there was by that sun made clear and warm and brave. And the Lady Arlynn put by her gown and her maidenhood with gracious, hungry rapture.

Before he took path with the Lady Arlynn, Kinch had had converse with Gro that he went to in puzzlement and love for the man he knew as Nim. And Gro's gray-green wolfish eyes were ever on Kinch as he told of what he knew of his Eigin mother Edwina and of her coming to Harold Holdering, King's Vicar in Southkirk, so close on Kinch's birth as to wag tongues, and to make him worry at his birthmark. And Kinch also told of his own time in Southkirk, until he and his mother were put down and made separate after Sorgun's raid and the Eigin name forbidden to men's lips.

And when his tale was in all essentials done, Gro put her hand that was ambered by mountain sun upon his thigh. And she told her tale.

"Nim is the name he has here at the foot of Rach Soturn, and accords with his honor and his need, for those who put by some lordship or other worldly fealty to come among us oft take another name, and besides Eigin was made anathema and he was sworn and commanded by his liege lord and King to put aside the name and sway of Eigin, and by no words or contrivance admit that name or sway. Yes, before the Lothians came last year this man was Orthos Eigin, chiefest head of the Eigin families and lord in fee simple of the Eigin Hold of the rich farm-lands to the south and east of Firnis."

"Is he," said Kinch, "the Orthos Eigin that held fortelesse Rerek against the Lothians with but eighty men?"

"No, lad," she said, "he is the second Eigin in the main line to bear that name, for the house has always gone by pairs so, and he named your father Derwent, and so withal decided your name as well. He is your father's father.

"And when your father was poisoned by some Lothian assassin, the Eigin House was in disarray and your mother sent, as now looks with you just in her womb, to Harold Holdering that Southkirk might be fortified by Eigin name and substance. Folk knew not that Southkirk took both branch and seedling, and that was well as you might not have lived over long in Firnis with a claim to Eigin House both through your mother's collateral line and of line direct through your father. Direct even to your birthmark that was upon your father Derwent and upon his father Orthos, even as he showed you this day. And well it was that you grew to manhood in Southkirk, for I hear that Firnis has been a sorry ruck in these years, with the insolence of the Lothians and the enmities among the lords of the land and the wont of purpose bred by these new-hatched priests of the Eye. When the King last year cast out Eigin and swore your grandfather and the others to full anathema, 'twas but one more nail." And Gro was silent for a space and Kinch thought of his Master Nim that was Orthos Eigin and his father's father.

"I should," said Kinch, "have known him by his nose that is bent like an eagle's beak." Gro stroked her own nose and gave a glance at Kinch as if to say that this was even so of Kinch himself. Kinch asudden thought of his mother Edwina's aquiline features and deep blue eyes, and he saw in his mind how they were changed male and ancient in his father's father. And Kinch's eyes were water.

"He is," Gro said soft and even, "sworn by his liege lord to maintain by no words or contrivance or to admit to the Eigin name or sway. He is wont to say that one can only take so much instruction from indifferent nature. And if he, in his duty as seeing master, should have exposed aught of Eigin, perhaps he can understand this as no abuse of his liege oath, but I would in no way press him nor speak in any way of Eigin or kinship."

"But," said Kinch, "how come you to be able to tell me of these matters?" For Kinch was minded that while mayhap he alone of the Eigin had sworn no oath of anathema, Gro, as head of a place that took its sustenance from Firnis, must have been sent the King's ban on the Eigin.

"Shush, lad," cackled Gro, "you have no need to twitch your nose after such of my honor as remains in my four score years." Then she added more gravely, "Nim, or Eigin, has been long a warrior clansman and liegeman to Firnis. But I am the servant to this place of seeing and no king's will may bite on me." Now she put her finger to his lips as one who will have no more words and she said, "I expect that you are soon for the road. I think the Master Nim awaits you in his cell."

And he bade Kinch enter when Kinch came to his cell, and in those spare quarters Kinch saw naught but a small bottle of wine and two earthenware goblets that rested on a study table between two stools. Butler's instruction now served Kinch well for he guessed from the look of it that this was the manhood ritual wine that he had last drunk in a silver cup from the hand of Harold Holdering, Vicar of Southkirk, that he then thought his father. Had

Kinch not so guessed, the bite of the resin might have set him spluttering for the wine was thick with it. After he tasted well Master Nim put his lips together as one who has tasted the tart persimmon and he said to Kinch, "Perhaps a few months past its time but all the better savor for it."

For the better part of the first hour after noon, they talked as Kinch and Master Nim. But gradually Kinch brought their talk round to the situation of Southkirk, of Trajus' conundrum and the Lothian raids. Kinch talked on a space so alone and then fell into silence.

And now came a grim precision into the voice that was his father's father, and Orthos Eigin said, "Keep you a careful watch on the priests of the Eye. They first appeared half a hundred years ago, along with the beginnings of the ills of the Salian Kingdom. 'By the oracles of the Eye that sees all and tells naught but truth,' has been with us but that span of time. And they're damnably right in what they say of events only hours or one or two days hence, as when tenth moon last they called out in Firnis that Sorgun had fallen upon the wheatlands and they called out so some six hours before the fastest horse from Mittol brought in this very intelligence.

"But what they say of more distant events is crabbed and riddlesome as when they said that Sorgun will stay in Firnis when next he comes, which may be read to mean that Sorgun will come as a peaceful ambassador when next he comes and so will come into Firnis, or it may be read to mean that Sorgun will storm Firnis itself when next he comes in arms, or it may be read in half a dozen other dark and unsettling ways. The priests of the Eye have some secret tie with Sorgun. And there's another small mystery of that black-cowled crew that needs some airing."

Now the old man brought forth a circular medal of ilgras, the milky-white jewel that fetches a score of times its weight in gold and is like that metal in being soft and yet incorruptible. And he laid the ilgras that had strange runes upon its surface in front of Kinch and he said, "This is what their chiefest priests wear privily upon the chest as a secret token of authority. And mayhap it makes them the dreary milksops that they be. For true it is that ilgras came to Salia in the time that brought the black-cowled folk, and that has been since a dismal epoch.

"I would have you take it that you might play some trick upon them, did I not fear that its moon-ish aura might more likely play you false; and you and yours are not easily given to being sneak-in-the-nights. Some say these jewels are made from the moon itself and that the Eye of Eyes looks down from there." And he reached and held Kinch's hand for a time.

And then he smiled and asked Kinch one question more before they said full farewells. "Tell me," said the old man, his ancient eyes glittering gaily, "tell me of this marvelous animal that the Lady Arlynn brought to Southkirk with her. For no reason that I could name, I am a most attentive naturalist respecting the great pard." And Kinch set out all to his delight before he came way with the Lady Arlynn.

"You must go?" the Lady Arlynn said to Kinch, as shadows came into this glen that was theirs.

"Surely," he said, "I must make my way to Southkirk with the sun. There lies what I must do." And the Lady Arlynn put speech by for several heartbeats that she might say what she must.

"I doubt not," she said, "that those large duties are there, but mine eyes dazzle with our local loyalties, with the compact grammar of arm and thigh and hip that has been our argument. That and that we have slain men together and been comrades for some paces on the road." And she paused but put him by from speaking.

"But I," said she most firm, "but I shall be your willing bondsman will you but say you'll be as now when fortune puts us again together. And be there 'til that time some service I may do, you shall have this and gladly, my lord."

And he held her most gentle and said, "Give not your pledge so liberal, my lady, for I may not prosper in all this and end cut down in some chance foray, and mayhap I see too large a scope for my own self in this."

And she said, "What I have given, I have given."

And he said, "Then let us to the maps in the scroll room, for I would show thee a thing or two."

"As my lord would have it," said the Lady Arlynn, and her voice sounded like the finest wine glass struck, "but by your leave I would first survey again and more fully these local counties." And truly they took to this final proposal most heartily, for they came to the scroll room by the light of tapers.

XV

Kinch came down the Ham road to Southkirk in
the dusk. And he reported to Syljanus as the last
gentle that he had seen and went with Syljanus
to Hacmon and the Vicar. And Hacmon had of
Kinch that he had found the Lady Arlynn and had
had to do with brigands of the mountains and had
returned to Southkirk and his duty, and Kinch was
wary to say more and gaunt Hacmon read some
message in Kinch's eyes, for he sent Kinch straight
to the kitchen. But it was pitch dark ere ever Kinch
won free to talk with Trajus and Bug, and they told
him of the fearsome growth of the great pard, and he
could not come to the cage but with the new day's
sun.

And as the great pard gave him her amber eyes
and ambled forward and leapt yet again upon him,
Kinch was now minded that he had told small to

Nim-Eigin of the size of this creature. For it seemed
to Kinch that the great pard was twice the size that
he'd remembered and he had been gone from
Southkirk but a moon of days.

The sun glistened in the great pard's hairy coat as
she put by her leaping at him that she might lie and
eye him brightly in the light from the cell's close-
barred window, while she panted softly that she
might put by the heat of her long exercise with him,
and her pinkish tongue lolled between her teeth that
were white as freshest milk. He could smell her
scent, sweetly musky and urinous but without the
rankness of the tom. Far different the cell that she
had dwelt in while he had been in the mountains,
and where Bug had brought her meat, though perforce Bug had not opened the door of that cell, nor
removed the great pard's droppings. When Kinch
had come that morning with the sun, his nostrils
were ripe with heavy midden odors when he but
opened the bradded door that led from the Lord's
yard down into the dungeon. And the great pard,
her amber eyes at the spy hole, gave several musical barks when she saw that Kinch was come.

So the morning had had more of stable cleaning
than play. After enough thrusting and scuffling for
Kinch to know he still had some span of rulership
with the pard, he opened her cell and let her forth
into the warden's passage. She bounded and sniffed
and scratched and peered about most joyously, and
paws athwart the barred window, she looked most
attentive down · at the greenish sea that splashed

high against Southkirk Fort with the morning wind
and tide. And when it chanced that one particular
wave sent spume nearly to the lip of that window,
the great pard pulled back of a sudden and let fly at
it with a paw. Kinch contemplated her midden-
sodden cell with less gaiety.

But there was naught for it. So Kinch swept
another cell and strew dry straw in one end of it,
that it might be bed for her. And he had not to drive
her to this other cell, for she came while he busied
himself there. So he bestowed her there, not without
some leaping and barking on her side, and went to
fetch means for the cleansing of her middenish cell.
And Kinch was sore ashamed that he had given no
thought to this when he had gone off, that had left
this joyous brave animal to live in her own muck.

Though it struck him as a strange labor for him
who was now perforce a future of Eigin House, yet
he was minded of Trajus' maxim that better a good
kitchen karl than a bad king, and he was also
minded that even as a captain must be full intimate
with all the weapons that his men use, so must a
king be full intimate with all the tasks of his folk,
even to the cleansing of midden stables. And Kinch
was minded that there were other such sties that
wanted cleansing hereabouts, and in Firnis.

So Kinch put by Bug, that was just without the
dungeon door, and would not have him help with
the cleansing but would have Bug go on to the
stave-fighting exercises that Trajus and he had had
the karls at each morning. And the sun was an hour

of noon when Kinch had done with his cleansing
and had stalked out to the Ham through a thicket of
karls that had made rough-hewn but withal comradely
jest of his condition such as one who called out,
"Ho, tomcat, you have taken both ladies of the
south, is your secret your perfume or your body
paint?" and another, "Old muckhills will bloom at
last."

One called out, " 'Tis the great pard," and a
silence went through their laughter like a lightning
bolt unseasonable in a cloudless sky and then their
laughter kindled up anew and stronger than before
as by twos and fours they realized that all about
were happy that the great pard meant Eigin and that
Kinch and the beast below somehow might measure
in that equation. But Kinch straight went to the
Ham and splashed himself fresh and returned to the
great pard, for the great pard's collar was stretched
tight into the fur and flesh round her throat by a
month of food, and he had puzzled what to do
respecting the pard's collar and now would have to
act out his thought.

Though the great pard that lolled in the swath of
the near noonday sun had ceased her panting; Kinch
could still hear in his ears the slight hint of a cough
in that panting that might stem from the tightness of
her collar. As she lay there the collar was all but
vanished in the hairy fold of her throat. And one
could not see the leather or the brassy buckle that
Kinch had studied in her leapings at him in which
she seemed twice the size that he'd remembered

though much as playful as before. He was minded
to loosen the collar at least one notch and he wondered whether he might come so intimate with her
and yet have her do him no damage, for he knew
that the throat was ever where one must come who
would do secure damage to a cat and so where one
must come who would do lordship with this most
brave of animals.

But there was naught for it. And so Kinch came
forward toward the great pard across the cell on his
knees, his arms and palms with fingers spread set
forward as one who would wrestle and knew the
level on which his opponent would oppose him. The
great pard rose and came at him and Kinch could
see that she would not leap at him for she ambled
forward slowly and her ears were up.

Then Kinch lowered his head to her level and put
down his hands upon the floor as though he was
minded to be as much cat as he could. And truly
Kinch could not have given a clean account of why
he did this thing, for it was no part of his strategy
but some form of not seeing and his hands moved of
their own or the floor raised itself to them and
Kinch's will had no part of it. The great pard brushed
smoothly by Kinch's head, and Kinch felt the fine
bushy fur of her head against his and her whiskers
bent along his cheekbones and her breathy muzzle
eased by his lips. And the great pard turned graceful and came once more toward him and their heads
came together once more in this comradely caress.
They did this thing thrice more, and with the final

pass Kinch heard clear what he first thought illusion
or the sounding sea, a low, gruff, rumbling purr.

And her amber eyes met his blue, and for a brave
moment Kinch felt as truth literal what the jesting
karl had said of him that he was a great pard,
though the karl had said so on the occasion of
Kinch's slain body and his other midden reek-
ing and had said that pard to signify that Kinch
was Eigin, and the folk about laughed to witness
this covert crowning.

But the brassy buckle must be loosened and the
tine of that buckle must move one notch in the
leathern collar and the tongue must return all secure under the lip of that buckle, and he athwart
the hot gates of her jaws the while he did this most
threatening intimacy. She let him to her side and he
brought both hands to her throat that he be speedy
and he eased round the buckle to the back of her
neck but he did so as one who would stroke and
groom. She paced forward a paw or two and Kinch
moved with her, his hands still at her collar that
now was tight as a noose. When he slipped forth the
tongue from the buckle, there came something of a
hiss into her voice and she would draw her neck
down and away from his hands. But Kinch was
minded that this best be done quick and on the first
essay, and he kept his fingers to their work and he
pulled back firm and to the right, that the tine be
out its hole. And he made to slide the tine into the
next hole but she swung forward quick, her head
still lower and her mighty muscles of her back

arched up her shoulders beneath him and she near turned her head beneath her haunches and withal pulled away from him and the collar with a snarl.

Now it was Kinch's thought that while it was good that the collar no longer choked her, the collar a notch looser must return now to her throat or she would never let it there again. So Kinch went again to her side and stroked and groomed the fur on her back and then on her throat where the collar had matted it. And into these caresses he slipped the collar round her throat and brought the tongue within the buckle and closed it quick until the tine slid in its proper hole, but as he did this thing the great pard lunged forward as before and Kinch fell upon her back like a wrestler, and held with all the strength that was in the great muscles of his shoulders and arms as his fingers shot home the tongue through the lip of the buckle. But now he had to do with the full fury of the animal.

Kinch could not ever have said later if he did best to cling to her collar, and to strive to keep his left hand at her collar atwisting for mastery, that ever that hand held her firm at the back of her neck so that he might hold her teeth off from him and from that arm. Had he thrust her off and leapt for his corner, he might have thrown off her first rushes and her temper soon to cool. But Kinch clove to her collar.

That she might not rip him with her claws, he clung round her back and back legs and held her to the floor, and he brought his right hand round under her right foreleg and thence to anchor in the fur and skin where throat met collarbone, and all the while she writhed a thousand ways and made to bite and claw at him, but Kinch held to her like iron.

Be it the instant eternity that it seemed to Kinch or an hundred heartbeats as the rest of the world knows time, the great pard put by her furious movements and fell awheezing, and then panting as Kinch let some little slack in her collar. Now Kinch saw that the hair under her throat and over her breastbone was dyed ruddy with blood. It came to Kinch that this could not be the great pard's blood and so Kinch by degrees understood that his hands and arms were smeared and adrip with blood. Her claws had done several shallow gashes upon his arms and that what might have been a glancing slash of canine had opened the middle finger of his right hand to the bone from knuckle to knuckle.

And several minutes now went by as Kinch stage by stage loosened his hold upon the great pard and as her muscles became less taut beneath him and she put by the hiss and the snarl and was quiet. After a time he gently stroked her side and belly and muzzle with the thumb and first finger of his right hand and but touched her collar with his left hand. It was as Kinch stood up and off from her that he came to know his greatest hurt, for at some juncture the great pard had had half her jaw round Kinch's right knee, and on either side of the meat of muscle just above that knee there were neat holes that through their depth and narrowness bled but sluggishly and Kinch could see the fibrous muscle and the whitish fat.

Still, this were no time to put by advantage won and Kinch knew what he must do.

So Kinch put himself once more upon his hands and knees, and the great pard came once more to him and they bumped and rubbed heads together. And Kinch came then once more to her side and heard her purring, and he rubbed her throat and smooth went from that to slipping the tongue from the buckle, the tine from its hole, and the collar from her throat.

She circled the cell once and then he came by her side and slid the collar once again around and had it snug together without more ado. He offered her his left hand in a fist and she licked at it. But he did not offer her his right which now ached most abominably in the middle finger, that was a mess of blood. And he thought that she was a brave animal that should do so merry with someone who must have appeared to her but late as one determined to throttle the life from her. Her purr was a sweet melodious rumble in his ears.

And Kinch backed to the cell door, and he knew of a sudden that he had not only to settle with pain but was weary and atremble, and to that he must add gaunt Hacmon who awaited him at the spy hole that looked in upon the cell from without in the warden's passage.

"I have," said Hacmon when Kinch came through the door, "seen men teach the saddle to wild horses caught from the Brineheld wastes. But 'til these past few minutes I had not seen a cat of this size, nor a great pard, nor one marshalled so to his master's lessons."

And now Hacmon, that had not the blunt nose nor girth of his younger cousin, the Vicar, but shared with him brown hair and curly beard, started for he saw that Kinch was clotted and adrip with blood. And Hacmon sat Kinch on a stool and took a clean rag that had gone unused in Kinch's scouring and he bound up Kinch's middle finger with a portion and he wound the rest round Kinch's knee.

"By what token," said Kinch, "do you know it to be a great pard?"

"I could," said Hacmon, "quote the authority of Southkirk's market, that is absolute it be a great pard, save those who will have it a lion dyed with spinach. And they argue if they be honest like Kindrel the poet, for it is so poetical that a herald's emblem of a house should in form physical as a great pard come together with the house itself, which is to say you, Kinch. And true it is what the Vicar says, that if Southkirkers see beauty in this conjunction, this makes it a strength, for folk are ever more ready to fight for diamonds than gravel."

And Hacmon looked Kinch straight in the eye and he said, "For me, I say it is a great pard because it is a great pard, as evidenced by its outsize paws and head, that are ever a sign that the animal has more to grow, and by its color, that goes to dun olive much as what we are told of the great pard, and no other cat or pard of this run of sizes with such a color."

Hacmon then smiled at Kinch and added, "If more be asked, I'd invoke your authority. For even my son Syljanus' recent rupture with the Vicar's overweening bully, Elgar, attests to your good offices. Since this past year has shown you to be no fool, you must think that it is a great pard, for otherwise you would not here force your suit on her in such bloodily intimate manner."

And Kinch wondered what tart draught this sweet talk presaged, for Hacmon was as one who soon must speak some difficult sentences. But the great muscles of Kinch's heart beat no faster, for his mind had put on the nimble calm of the runner who has just come a winner from a long foot race. "There may come a time I shall press other suits," said Kinch, "but truly, my Lord Hacmon, this instant I am happy as a hummingbird."

"The Vicar," said Hacmon, "will make you an officer within a space. 'Tis honor and policy both. And would do this thing now but that Elgar is wild now in council and ever will throw Eigin in the Vicar's face." And in his part, gaunt Hacmon spoke to the wall. "The ban," said Hacmon, "that sent your lady mother to Anticore convent was most explicit and unbending, and it was under the King's seal and we've had most steady assurances from Firnis that it is indeed the King's will however much it troubles him. If the King a time or thrice pays the Price to keep the Lothians from making a

bonfire of our harvest and home, this may be plain
wisdom, and the Price may not be in gold and silver
and ilgras alone but sometime a name must be laid
low. But it is not our part as liege men to bicker
with the King's will but to make strong our space of
the land. The Vicar was no more free in this than
when Firnis sent him your maiden Eigin mother as
bride and you in her womb." With this last, Hacmon
looked round at Kinch.

And Kinch looked steady into Hacmon's eyes,
and then nodded once as one who will say go on.

"You know of this then?" said Hacmon.

"And that he who fathered me, Derwent Eigin,
had most like been poisoned by some agent of
Lothia."

"Then," said Hacmon, "part of what weighs down
the Vicar is already put aside. But surely you did
not learn this by word of the Lady Edwina?" And
Hacmon stumbled over her name as one whose grief
wells up when his lips first again essay a name.

"Not from her," said Kinch.

"She and the Vicar were compact from before
your birth that you not be told until such a time that
you reached manhood and were known to be dis-
creet and that it was needful that you know. For
neither wished that you be the principal quarry for
Eigin haters and a boy is no happy choice to burden
with dark secrets. And is it not true, Kinch, that
until last year's ban, the Vicar honored and loved
you as his son and even as he so honored and loved
Elgar that was his own blood?"

"Even so," said Kinch, and the Vicar's blunt features and curly beard of brown and gray came to Kinch's mind, that had not made this face for a time. "What may I do?" said Kinch.

"Kinch," said Hacmon, "there are things more convenient to a karl than to a King or his Vicar or the officer of his Vicar. Look to the priests of the Eye to see if they do some secret mischief to Southkirk, for they have prophesied that Sorgun will stay in Firnis when next he comes."

"So," said Kinch, "you came here to tell me something of my genealogy and that I will be an officer when it is politic and that the Vicar is still bound by the King's ban to have no converse with me?"

"No," said Hacmon, "I was to speak with you about a thing or two that it might be determined how much to tell you of this, and that you should be told to look to the black-cowled."

"So," said Kinch laughing, "you have made this determination by speaking with me and have told me all?"

" 'Twas not," said Hacmon, "by speaking, nor did I determine of it, for the Vicar decided on it and he did not hear you speak. We came together to this dungeon that you might see I came from him direct and then he was to leave while I spoke with you about a thing or two, and we were then to determine whether to go further. We watched you with the great pard when you played with her and when you put forth your strength against her. And he said when he left and just before you came forth from the cell, 'I do not know the language that they speak together but he is most damnably eloquent in it. There is no need to jabber with him about a thing or two. Tell him all and straightway.' "

The great pard barked cheerily as they came forth from the dungeon. And a small group of gentles and freedmen at the far end of the Lord's yard started to see gaunt Hacmon clasp Kinch in grave farewell as if Kinch were a lord and Hacmon's equal. Though then Hacmon went in to the Vicar's chamber in the Lord's apartments and Kinch limped to the kitchen and its duties.

XVI

When Kinch came out of his sleep to see the stones of the great pard's cell, lit milky white by the full moon, they looked for a moment to be a fortune of precious ilgras. Though it was hard for him to feel enchanted by these stones, thinly strewn with straw, that had made the side on which he slept cold and stiff. There was more than a finger of winter in the air though the harvest season had just begun. He fancied that his knee ached where the great pard had bit him, though the wounds had healed and but pale scar-skin marked their place, and he had been running at dawn and stave-fighting for weeks. The knee might also ache from the strain he had put upon it that he might hold firm and silent amid the rafters of the temple over the dais where the High Priest of the Eye gave audience and privately incanted to his jewel.

A month had passed since first he had begun to spend time in and around the place of the priests of the Eye. Their temple was a brightly painted, ramshackle oblong, high-roofed at the inner end, that had been a merchant's warehouse until the black-cowled priests had bought it a dozen years ago. They had shored up its central beams, furbished its interior with draperies and a maze of initiate cells and consultation booths and chapels, painted the outer walls saffron yellow trimmed in crimson and purple. Then they set achanting to four thousand gods and goddesses, making spirit readings, and on occasion issuing, under the grim authority of the Eye, bleak statements that folk had come to recognize as true albeit niggardly riddlesome in some particulars. The chanting, having somewhat the quality of a battalion of cats in rut taught to howl in rough unison, was unloved by the folk of the Bear tavern and the nearby merchants. The spirit readings were most done by first degree initiates who wore not black but gray cowls. And these readings were held in general account to be in no marked way better than those of the fortune tellers of the market and withall somewhat lacking in color and savor. But a statement from the Eye, issued from the front of the temple by a black-cowled priest standing under the direction of the High Priest: That did folk greet with much of the respect given an edict from Firnis under the King's seal. And so did folk shudder when the Eye said that Sorgun would stay when next he came to Firnis, though they were unsure how to understand these words.

After several days of fitful attempts, Kinch came to chant well enough to satisfy the initiates. They began to pay him less attention. Thus he might reduce the wind that he pushed through his throat and so put off the hoarseness that the high-pitched, raucous chanting bred. And once their attention was afield, Kinch could listen, during pauses in the chanting or while meditating, to what came to pass in the spirit-reading booths.

Kinch came to listen to Novice Hind's readings in particular. The wiry young man with large brown eyes and long lank black hair did his readings in a clear high voice and he did those readings in the leftmost recess of a line of booths, where just beyond it was most plausible that Kinch might meditate or chant. For there Kinch could sit at the edge of a small chapel. A mostly unused chapel for there within the shouts, songs, and yeasty babblings of the Bear were ever in the ear. And further, Kinch soon came to suspect and then to know that Novice Hind cared little that Kinch would listen to his art, eventually even onto inducting Kinch into the reading.

After some afternoons Kinch came to see that those who would have the sticks read for them fell into three or four sorts. Four if one counted those who came pushed by their comrades who paid the incense price.

As befit such matters spiritual, the reading had

no price, but ever it was that the client began by placing an incense cone in the earthenware dish in front of the reader. Incense bought from a novice under the eye of a black-cowled priest for a brass obel, the price of the two large tankards of beer that were a better and more nourishing way to enlightenment if the patrons of the Bear were to be believed. Said to come from the Southern Empire but boiled up in nearby Moor End, the oily black incense brought in enough to feed the dozen novices and five priests.

Those who were pushed forward by their comrades were a trouble to Novice Hind, for oft they did not know or trust the sticks. And oft they had no question that troubled them, and they were fearful and tongue-tied withal. So was it with the moon-faced lad that Kinch watched first, who, half carried in by his comrades and set down in front of Novice Hind, gave no answer to the stock opening, "Have you need to know what the sticks say?" Novice Hind had shooed the companions away, and took the incense cone from the lad's clenched hand and lit it. When he repeated his question, the lad goggled his eyes and tried to speak but all that came from his lips was a wheezy sound. When Hind offered him the sticks, Hind's hand covering the runes, the moon-faced lad's hand shook so that Hind must make selection for him, and when Hind threw the sticks sharply down for the reading, the lad fainted. Kinch helped the shaken Hind revive him.

Far different was it with those who came, as did most, driven by their own hopes and fears. Many of these had hopes and fears of love, others of trade, and some, seemingly, of all things. For each the Novice Hind would speak of the runes and of the fall of the sticks upon each other. Withal, through nods and startled glances and agreeing words, the Novice would discover somewhat of the client's life. And then he'd tell this tale back to the client, as though this local history were written in the sticks. Most folk find themselves a matter worth lengthy survey, so the wiry Novice with long straight black hair did not tell the tale over quick, that it might with the more starry-eyed require several sessions and several cones of incense for the telling.

It was so with the straw-haired garrison soldier's woman who came once again to Novice Hind the night before Kinch found himself in the great pard's cell. Her protacted worries returned ever to her soldier lover, by name Wirt, who appeared a find most fair but was forgetful and in some measure shy. Though the woman was long promised marriage by the worthy Wirt, it appeared that as one of Southkirk's stout defenders he must have the leave of the captain general that he marry—and that he sleep on occasion outside the garrison barracks that sat within and under the southmost wall of the fort.

Wirt had waited for some space of moons the arrival of Trajus, that he might ask his leave. But Trajus captained but a day and proved as the haggard eagle that outgoes his master's command—and cast down blinded and hamstrung, poor gentle. Sithence, so sorrowed the straw-haired woman, there had been no captain general in Southkirk. And gaunt Lord Hacmon that was elder cousin to the Vicar had the duties of the post. But Wirt was shy to go for leave to Hacmon who was not in name captain general and who was a Lord and withal of the Vicar's blood. Further, Wirt had left Southkirk that very day with a force of more than an hundred, more than half the garrison. All this force was led by Lord Hacmon down the great southern road through the southern fens and waste that lead to Lothia, that he might leave a dozen warriors well posted to warn of a raid by cursed Sorgun. And, though Wirt had assured her that the Lothians would not come araiding until the harvest was done and that some weeks in the future, she worried that Wirt should be caught up by some fennish ague on the road, or have the pox from some Lothian slattern, or be sorcelled by demons of the waste, or be left as a lonely sentinel while the rest of the garrison returned. And there was a widowed shopkeeper who had been a friend to her father in days gone by.

All this did not come from the straw-haired young woman in ordered account, but in crumbs and slivers, while the Novice Hind read from the sticks. Nor did the Novice seem to seek any of this from the woman. Thus Novice Hind would see the stick whose runes signified a broken sword lying near another that signified a river and so a journey or a decision or a course of life. Then, with some show of resistance,

Hind would admit that the broken sword might mean the wooden staves that the warriors and karls must flail about with and break upon large shields of afternoons, that her time with Wirt be less.

And Novice Hind was driven to admit that the broken sword might also signify the mysterious brave young lord of unnameable ancient family who led these exercises. A lord who, so Wirt had assured her, dressed as a karl and did kitchen duties, that he might conceal himself from the evil spells of the sorcerers of Rach Nord. Yes, and though it was clear that the river was the Ham and the journey was Hacmon's excursion toward Lothia, a deeper look might reveal that in its triple aspect the broken sword was also Wirt, who might put by war for a time and enjoy the softer joys of love. This reading was still more likely in that Wirt had near broken his foot with one of the clumsy wooden practice shields, that were the shape and size of doors—and this all silliness, quoth Wirt, for such a shield could never be carried on horseback in real war.

Still, insisted Novice Hind, the two sticks rest next to the rune of the rock pillar and the rune of the coin that signified age and commerce. And so the broken sword might mean that she would give up Wirt for the widowed shopkeeper.

But the straw-haired woman, whom Kinch thought but a girl before she spoke, pressed Novice Hind to find a definite choice in the sticks, that she might know whether her tomorrows lay with Wirt or the shopkeeper. And she turned to Kinch, who sat nearby as though in meditation at the edge of chapel alcove. She did not know him as the mysterious brave young lord of Wirt's account.

"And you, priest," she said to him, "can you see further?" And Kinch made a show of returning from his trance and attending to the fallen sticks, while he sought what he might do, for he would not offend the Novice. And the Novice Hind smiled and bid him speak his wisdom. And Hind spoke as one confident that he had read most of a message, and eager to hear should some small point be found to add to it.

"I am not a skilled reader of the sticks," said Kinch, after he had made to study their configuration for a time. "But at times they are clear enough for even such as I. In your future there is both a man of swords and a man of coins. And the river stick that signifies a journey must mean that you cannot now make a choice, but all will be resolved in the space of days or weeks, as in a journey." Kinch held his face still, for the somber face of wisdom that the Novice put on changed for a heartbeat to a wink.

And when the straw-haired woman turned back to him, the Novice Hind said, "It is because you wish to wait no longer but must do so that the sticks speak so clearly of a space of time, of a journey, of a river, before all is resolved."

"But I am so much in doubt," she said. And Kinch saw that her eyes were awatered and her face trembled and was alive with the softness of youth, though her chin was absent somewhat in the manner of the turkey bird.

"The fates must not be pushed," said Kinch, "for plainly the sticks say wait." Kinch watched her back as she left the temple and he felt some bitter taste within his mouth, though he felt that she had best wait, however the sticks fell upon the Novice's board. And Kinch reflected that if the sticks were a mirror, a mirror that said the tale back to the teller, human made as good a glass as sand. "Come," he said to the Novice, "the day is hot and talk dry and temple air dusty with wisdom. Let us cleanse our throats." And the Novice Hind said yea and a smile sped across his face below his spacious liquid brown eyes.

And so it was that Kinch came forth two hours of midnight from the Bear, the Novice Hind safely bestowed behind in beery sleep, his knowledge of the innards of the temple absorbed and his gray novice's cloak round Kinch. When the Bear quieted, the rest of Southkirk's folk were most long abed. The street and nearby shops and warehouses dark and even the saffron yellow of the temple of the priests of the Eye looked dim gray and the crimson was black. Kinch ambled up the steps and entered the temple past a half-sleeping novice who followed his gray cloak with a dull gaze. The novices and three of the priests slept in the alcoves along the right side. But the High Priest and his two close aides had rooms further back. Kinch slipped behind the draperies as he moved into the temple's innards.

Elgar had named him Kinch when he went behind the draperies of the eating hall in Fortress Southkirk. He must take care to be hidden. The name did in no way bite upon him now. Eigin he was by blood, Kinch he was for these times. And a kinch was a noose, even as the hempen rope adorned the gray weathered gibbet without the town of the year's end assizes.

Kinch slipped through the temple darkness to the far end with no more noise than a well rewarded royal house karl might make fetching a fine midnight draught to secret gentle lovers. Behind the altar of the central chamber he came through draperies to the door of the chamber of the High Priest. There was a faint light beneath the door but no sound within. And then, heart pounding within his house bones, Kinch slipped back within the bluish draperies, for a priest came bearing a bright burning taper.

The priest tapped upon the High Priest's door. The priest said something of the hour and the oily voice within said, "I am always ready for my Lord's call whatever be the hour. Come within and tell me all."

As the door shut, Kinch put her ear upon it but could not hear the words they said within, though he could hear the rise and fall of the sounds. But he knew from the Novice Hind that the space of the High Priest's inner chamber stretched upward to the roof. The muscles and strings of his frame were strained to the uttermost ere ever he won silently

through the blackness to the rafters above the High
Priest. He listened out of the dark above them. Ill
fortune, thought Kinch, that their talk was most
done. And the vital part of it given way to stale
news and market chat. The oily voice of the High
Priest seemed more to speak to the High Priest
himself than to the other priest.

"Over an hundred of the garrison trotting off with
Lord Hacmon at dawn this morning means they'll be
nesting halfway along the fens by now. A less ener-
getic captain might have risen at noon and camped
at dusk hardly south of the Ham. But Hacmon is
well away. Far from Southkirk and the Ham and the
Cut and the sea." The High Priest paused.

"Does the Eye see danger for Lord Hacmon and
his men?" asked the young priest.

"Enough, lad. The Eye speaks only when it wishes
even though one so humble as I implore it. It is
silent even for you that have been priest for the
whole of a year." And now the High Priest paused
again. "You did right, brother, to come straight to
my chamber with this message from the man. Yes,
the man wore the medallion rightfully. I assure you
he was a High Priest of the Eye, albeit he seemed
strange to you, for some of our most worthy brothers
cannot wear the black cloak in the open. And I say
worry not for Hacmon and his men, for you know it
is too early in the season for the Lothians to be on
the road. Take a measure of the commissary brandy
and compose yourself for sleep."

Kinch held himself arched rigid and still when

the young priest withdrew. And so he heard when
the High Priest hissed to himself. "Better to have to
do with bloody Sorgun roaring for his virgin bridal
gift of Lady Arlynn than with this ass abaahing.
Even an ass should guess that Hacmon is safe down
the road for now. Safer than he'd be in the streets of
Southkirk. There may be Lothians on the road in a
score of days but they will not be there now." The
High Priest fell silent and knelt down. And now
Kinch must think of how he would swivel from his
perch to a nearby beam, and so along it to the front
of the temple. As he sought to move he was near to
falling, for a thigh muscle long held rigid spasmed
as he made to shift his weight toward the beam.

The High Priest below brought forth from his
gown his ilgras medallion and held it all reverently
in his hand, and chanted to his god. "Southkirk will
know thy will, O Lord." As Kinch eased more
quickly back along the beam he heard the chant
finally change. "Ever Thy bidding will be done,
even at dawn as it is at midnight." Kinch came forth
like a cat from the temple. Fifty paces from that
building, he laughed and ran to the marketplace
fountain, that he might wash the film of incense
from his face. But when he returned to Fort
Southkirk's kitchen, his gentle knockings did not
rouse anyone within. They'd had feast in the great
hall that night, passing Hacmon's cup, and now
karls slept soused as gentles.

He heard gravel scrape near the postern gate.
Lord Elgar, the Vicar's heir that was late his elder

brother, slipped into the first door of the Lord's apartments. He had not been at the Bear, nor did he move as one who had drunk deep. Perhaps Elgar had put quit to another lust in the cribs at the far end of the docks.

Rather than pound further, Kinch turned away. Of a sudden the romance of the night held him. And the newly risen moon shone down from the east and a little of the north, and its beams made a shimmer of the Lord's yard.

So came Kinch to sleep in the great pard's cage for the night. For he had heard from the Lady Arlynn that those who kept falcons in the Southern Empire would sleep a night in chamber with their falcons so that they might gain a greater bond with them. Though the great pard barked and made some play with Kinch, he calmed her. Thus sleep it was and soon, for Kinch was sore weary. And it was not the hard stones, lightly strewn straw, that awakened him in that dismal time two hours before dawn. Nor was it the cold, nor the light of the setting moon that lit the stones a milky white like ilgras. No, it was the great pard, that had her forepaws upon the ledge of the cell's window, and looked out into darkness of the Cut. Black against milk quartz in the window, her head and shoulders were as dark night itself, diamonded where the moonlight shimmered here and there along her mantle. The great pard was growling.

And Kinch saw, in the slip below the Fort at the beginnings of the docks, two long boats. The nearest one bobbed empty. The second, oars just now raised from a last stroke, was as full of black-clothed Lothian warriors as a pomegranate with seeds. And even as Kinch asked himself where might be the contents of the first boat, the warriors of the second came rapidly and silently ashore.

XVII

Then from the shadows of the Fort came silently a huge man whose coarse blond hair spilled over the gorget of his blackened leather, brass-bossed breast armor. "Damned to perdition be the pilot," he hissed, "who steered you in that backwash. We've made way to the Vicar's chamber with nary an outcry, for they be swollen drunk with sleep. And we'll have that stubborn swine here in a thrice if you'll but follow me to hold the way. Torun has his blade on his throat and will kill the Vicar if we cannot bear him forth convenient for hostage." But Kinch had the great pard's chain in his left hand and the singing sword in his right. And that man and that fearsome great amber-eyed cat made no sound as they paced across the dark yards toward the entrance to the Lord's apartments that was next to the postern gate.

Kinch remembered nothing from the time he heard
Sorgun's words to the time he plunged through the
door of the Vicar's larger sleeping chamber. Kinch
did not remember passing the strangled guard on
the stairs beyond the entrance near the great hall
and the postern gate. Nor could he remember thinking that the Vicar would most like be in this larger
chamber, convenient to the great hall after an evening of revelry. Nor could he remember debating
stratagems, that he might face a room of armed
men. But the singing sword and the great pard
proved most substantial arguments.

Lord Sorgun's sworn lieutenant, Torun, had his
blade a finger's width from the Vicar's throat. And
his left hand held the Vicar's right arm taut behind
his back. Weather-faced grizzled Torun was of the
grim fighting men from round Rerek in the Lothian
horselands. His father and his father's father had
died for Sorgun and Sorgun's line. Had he been
alone and had Kinch plunged through the door with
a squad of heavily armored warriors, Torun would
have opened the Vicar's throat wide and then flung
himself on his enemies. But when Torun saw the
great pard and saw the great pard's master, blond-
haired and beak-nosed, hushed tales heard in child-
hood welled up around him. Surely this were some
maddish specter from the Pit, like were come alive
the master of the skeletal black ruin of fortelesse
Rerek, that were a graveyard horror of Lothian these
hundred years. The face that was that of Eigin grew
large in his vision and palpable. For his blade was

swept roofward from his nerveless fingers by singing
steel. And he breathed, "Eigin," and he died.

As Torun fell in a heap before him, all became
slow and clear for Kinch. The great pard crouched
just behind him, atop a black-clad Lothian at whose
throat the pard had supped. That Lothian's sword
still pointed at Kinch. The four others stared at the
olive-gray great pard, who snarled and raised her
paw at them. And the great-bodied, grizzle-bearded
Vicar grinned across Torun's body at Kinch. The
Vicar had caught Torun's longsword as it had fallen.
"The man," he said to Kinch, "knows the quality of
a lord. And if he say Eigin, while I must say Kinch,
I know quality as well."

Kinch smiled and gestured with the singing sword
toward the four who stood on the far side of that
chamber. He gestured as one who would ask *Shall
we?* "Let's carve them, lad," said the Vicar with a
bearish voice.

But as Kinch so gestured he saw that there were
but three black-clad Lothian warriors and the fourth
was Elgar, that was son of the Vicar. The tallest
held his blade nearby Elgar as though he would
guard Elgar as Torun had the Vicar but his grip was
slack as he looked at the swords of Kinch and the
Vicar. Now this tallest Lothian turned to Elgar,
almost as one who would ask council. The other two
Lothians came forward toward the Vicar and Kinch,
their longswords on guard. Kinch saw that he might
not come direct to Elgar's aid so he threw the
singing sword at the tall Lothian. And though the

sword hit handle first, it hit the Lothian square in the stomach, and the breath was knocked from him and he fell backwards across a dais, his sword clattering to the floor.

The Vicar, whose swarthy face was now ruddy, bore back his man's sword with two thundrous heavy blows, smashing his collar bones and crushing him to the floor with the third. And the scar-faced Lothian veteran who came for the swordless Kinch reckoned not with the great pard who came upon him as lightning, knocking him asprawl and ripping with her rear paws at his stomach and thighs, while her jaws and forepaws held his shoulders and neck in deadly embrace.

The Vicar's face was first a comradely smile to Kinch. Then his face grew stern and wrought with pain, as one who must cut the flesh from his limb's end, that the whole might not blacken and die. "Who led the way to my chamber?" he thundered.

The Vicar had turned to the tall Lothian, who looked up from his helpless sprawl at Elgar and his own sword that Elgar held. And Elgar hewed down at the Lothian in that instant of time in which the Vicar shouted, "Kill him not!"

Now all that were alive in that chamber stood as of a sudden still like statues, though one might hear their breaths coming in labored gasps. The Vicar's stern and pain-wrought face now filled with blood. "How did they know their way to my chamber?" said the Vicar. His voice was like a fury from the

Pit held tight in iron chains. And under his eyes, Elgar's face turned yellowish pale like buttermilk.

"I would," said the Vicar to Elgar, "have had this Lothian's answer to that question. No need. For I see my answer in your traitorous face, cur. Did Sorgun promise that he'd kill me in the end, that you be his Vicar? Or did he but offer a share of my hostage price?" And at each terrible word grew Elgar's eyes more desperate.

Now Kinch saw Elgar grasp at his throat and pull forth an ilgras medallion such as he had seen the High Priest chant at. And, just as had the High Priest, Elgar said, "Southkirk will know thy will, O Lord." But though he said these words with the odd chanting rhythm of the High Priest, Elgar said these words as quickly as tongue might move. As he began them again, Kinch leapt forward at him.

Elgar turned aside, so Kinch came upon his back, and brought both his hands under and around Elgar's shoulders, Kinch's fingers knitting together behind Elgar's neck. Kinch heard a muffled voice, as though the ilgras medallion held a jinn inside, say, "Sorgun harkens." And Kinch hissed, "Say not a word," in Elgar's ear.

But Elgar could not keep mum. He shrieked, "Sorgun, they have—" But there was no more of Elgar's sentence, for Kinch bent forward his hands most powerfully and he felt strings lengthen and snap, and the bones of Elgar's neck that would curve no more were winched from their accustomed order and Elgar's body gave one great spasm and was still.

And now the Armorer was at the door with an officer and some several men, all naked from their beds with but longswords and sometimes shields. The Armorer's torso hair was grizzled, and here and there his flesh sagged round his powerful muscles, but he stood with all dignity and said, "We came with the noise and have passed a dead man on the stairs." Now the Armorer's eyes drank in the contents of the Vicar's chamber, that was a charnel house of death, with alive but a giant beast and the karl, Kinch, who looked at him over the lifeless form of Elgar. The Armorer looked to the Vicar.

"The skilled hangman," said the Vicar to the wall over dead Elgar, "breaks the neck in the fall and is no strangler." The Vicar spoke to no one but himself, or to Elgar's spirit, if such there was. The Armorer looked Kinch full in the face. Both knew that Kinch meant noose. And the Armorer somehow remembered that Kinch was more master than karl. And now the Vicar, that must be Lord here, turned himself again to iron.

"Good Armorer," said the Vicar Harold Holdering, "do not fear the great pard, for this beast is our bosom sister. The nether beast, Lord Sorgun, and some handful of Lothians are without. Kinch here is your commander as my hand. Let us make them feel the teeth of Southkirk."

Kinch, the Vicar, and the Armorer and his half dozen met Sorgun just without the postern gate.

And though Sorgun and his five were outdone in
numbers, they all had armor and stood well the
charge of those of Southkirk, and the Armorer took
a slash across his grizzled chest. Sorgun and his
men formed a wall of swords and shields and armor,
and they gave way slowly, moving back all orderly
toward their boats. The Vicar and Kinch ever stormed
forward against Sorgun, the Vicar slashing great
strokes, and Kinch, the singing sword flying most
deft and swift, forming a shield for the twain. But
Sorgun and his veterans formed ever a wall, and one
that pulled back steadily, and true it was that the
Vicar's great strokes came less quick as his anger
cooled and his breath came labored.

Kinch surged forward as Sorgun's guard man turned
toward their boat. And Kinch swung the singing
sword a great two-handed stroke-heavenly down on
Sorgun's sword and shield. Sorgun's longsword shattered and the steel lip of his shield was opened by
the last force of Kinch's blow. Sorgun glared and
said, "And so the temper of my tool has failed. I
have others than the Vicar's son. Think not to awe
me with your night creature."

But now Lord Sorgun and his men were come
back to the five at their boat, and they leapt within
while two with bows loosed arrows at the men of
Southkirk. And as they rowed swiftly out the Cut,
Sorgun had but one satisfaction. As they reached
some ten horse-lengths in the water, the Vicar hurled
Torun's sword and it caught the collar of the pilot
that had earlier malsteered the sound, pinning the

pilot's neck down into the stern thwart. Sorgun
laughed but the laugh was not hearty. His voice was
a snarl when he said, "Then shall the Price be that
much more when our force is fully mustered."

The great pard snarled back at him from the
shore. Now the Lothians pulled upon their oars most
heartily, that they would come apace to their ship
without the Cut. And in the boat Sorgun most roughly
counciled his men that they should not say over-
much of that greenish battle mastiff of Southkirk.
Still less should they make of this material horror
some pardish nightmare. Sorgun was minded that
when he was in his private cabin he could use the
medallion to inquire after the blond-haired, hawk-
nosed youth in homespun who fought so well and
smashed Sorgun's longsword with a shorter weapon.
There was a look to that youth that Sorgun hoped
had gone unseen among his men. And so did Sorgun
first feel the teeth of Southkirk, that now as the
dawn sun looked upward from its lowest estate.

XVIII

The Armorer and his half-dozen men stood bemused to watch the Lothian boat quick rowed down the Cut and into the earliest glower of dawn. True it was they could not have put boat and oars in the water before the Lothians fetched their galley, that stood in shadow form on the horizon without the Cut. The Vicar took Kinch in his arms and kissed him upon both cheeks. And the great pard ever brushed her muzzle to and fro upon the chief muscle in Kinch's calf, and the great pard gave forth a rough and husky purr with each pass.

Kinch took the great pard's leather, and the Vicar and the Armorer and his men now took themselves back through the narrow postern gate of Southkirk, into the common yard. There folk were gathered all about, the two score of garrison and stragglers, and the more of the kitchen and the keep, those of the

Lord's apartments, and several of those that had slept in the great hall, some two hundred and more, and strangely for the dawn, an assemblage of Southkirk. The Vicar came to the center of those that were there collected. And the Vicar said in his great voice clapping Kinch upon his shoulder, "I will have this man Kinch for my captain general in this Fort of Southkirk." And the Vicar's eyes frankly surveyed this host that had collected about and the Vicar said unto them, "If any will not have this man as captain general, speak now."

Folk now looked about, but all eyes after a space came unto Kinch, who stood in simple kitchen garb within the respectful space that the great pard made about him. And folk marked the short sword that Kinch held, that shone like watery silver that is unscratchable and that had shattered Lord Sorgun's sword as an axe might seasoned kindling. Now Kinch looked the Vicar full and frank in the eye and Kinch said, "I may not be captain general, for I am Lord of the Eigin line, as well you know, my Vicar." And when Kinch said, Eigin silence came upon the crowd and all eyes were on the Vicar, whose face went white.

After the space of thirty heartbeats, the Vicar said, "I recognize your quality, though let me still call you Kinch as I did not hear your other name."

And Kinch said, "Kinch is enough. As what I am it is my duty plain to help defend this place of ours. And as you would have me look to the defense of Southkirk, even unto giving her a captain general, I will gladly tell you who should be our man. I'll name our captain general, and shall be the fingers of mine arm."

The Vicar looked at him for a time and then nodded. Now there was a silence in the air, that rose steadily upward from the cool courtyard into the dawn. This dawn sun cast, through the morning dew, full bright rays upon Kinch's face. And Kinch said, "I name Trajus as captain general in this Fort of Southkirk."

And as the sun, great brazen warmer, broke over the battlements of Southkirk, lightening one face or another, so was kindled here and there some nobility in those within the yard. So stoutly several shouted, "Trajus! We shall have Trajus!"

The Vicar's eyes glistened and he said softly to Kinch, "You have done noble work this night for Southkirk. Well I remember that she whose name I forget but nothing else, and was your mother, had Trajus swear an oath to you. So you do well to recall your man. As our bard Kindrel says, 'True lords need men as a lioness needs cubs.' How of his blindness?"

Kinch's blue eyes now held full the brown eyes of the Vicar. "I'll be his eyes for ordinary sights," said Kinch. "For the rest his eyes are keener than mine. And he has fought an hundred battles and he and his blood have ever been champions of my house."

"Though his legs' strings be cut," said the Vicar, "he can ride in some fashion."

"Perhaps," said Kinch with a smile, "we will think less of horseback these days."

Now folk stirred, for Butler and Bug approached, bearing blind Trajus between them. Folk wondered that he stood so tall. When he was brought to Kinch's side, the great pard purred and smelt of his legs and licked them, for ever at stave-fighting the great pard would stay at Trajus' feet while Kinch led the mêlée. Kinch put his arm round Trajus, embracing him. And folk whispered that Kinch, that was Eigin, now stood with the pard that was his house's sign and with blind Trajus, that seemed for many but risen from the dead.

"Will you, Trajus," said the Vicar in his great voice, "be my captain general in the hold of Southkirk?" Trajus looked toward the Vicar's voice and bowed and said, "I have ever done your service, and that of my lord, and that of Southkirk. So I am most happy to abide in mine office. And those warriors here about and those karls that will play, we shall talk this afternoon at staves. We must learn manners that we may serve Sorgun still more proper when next he comes."

The Vicar laughed loud and held Kinch's hand in both of his. And the Vicar said to Kinch's ear most soberly, "The time of the Price is past, for Sorgun will ask too much and the man will be bloody vengeful. And the priests of the Eye say that Sorgun will stay when next he comes. Your sword must work now. And I'll carve their guts if they win through your shield, lad."

A stoup of strong brown ale was brought at the order of the Vicar, that all might drink deep of it. And the folk about first shouted *Southkirk* by which they meant the Vicar and then they shouted *Kinch* still more loudly. The hairs on the back of the Vicar's neck rose up when he heard some folk shout *Eigin* amongst the other cries.

When Hacmon and his men returned from the south, they found that battle had been behind them. The Vicar retired that night early to his smaller chamber with a pair of bottles that had been salvage from Lady Arlynn's ship. And the Vicar drank the wine of those bottles and bit the middle finger of his right hand to the bone. Then he wrapped that finger in clean linen and fell into a deep sleep and rose all himself and lordly in the morning. And the straw-haired, weak-chinned maid did not wed the ancient merchant, but straightway called before Kinch she chose her military love. So Wirt slept without the garrison, though his bruises from the door-large shields were even greater. In those next several days did Kinch on occasion finger the ilgras medallion that he had taken from Elgar's throat, Kinch tempted to say to the jewel that chant of the High Priest that had been on Elgar's lips when he died. And Trajus, that was Kinch Eigin's man, was captain general once more in Southkirk.

XIX

"I would trust both of them," said Trajus from his canvas chair, where he held the ilgras medallion most delicate between his fingertips.

Kinch sprawled in the noonday sun, his back athwart one of the sweet-smelling new hay bales that lay for the morning at the edge of the common yard. The great pard slept by him, her head upon his thigh, and now and then came a soft whistle or hiccup in her slow-rhythmed sleeping breath.

"Syljanus," continued Trajus, "learns. He had pat the sense of the large shield. He is Hacmon's son and the farm lads of Hacmon's hundred will fight for him as well. And there's sober love for you in his voice, for you have scholared him well. Hacmon—with Syljanus under him—will be your right wing before the Ham. The Vicar in the center. The left must be your command direct. For Sorgun

and his horse will seek that way over. The road is
there, and the foothills, and it is farthest from
Southkirk."

"Sorgun," said Kinch, "is no old dog, as this sea
raid proves. Could take the unexpected side."

"No," said Trajus. "This recent assault leaves
tradition behind. But was secret within an inch of
victory. Sorgun will try no such gamble in the open
field where you may see his horse assemble for the
charge. You must dispose yourself on the left.

"This Novice Hind," continued Trajus, "loves
you too and soberly, albeit with much less cause
than Syljanus. For you made him drunken unto
sleep in the Bear and stole his habit and traduced
his temple. To your limited credit you helped him
with the mumbo jumbo of stick-reading for Wirt's
bride. You called him here this dawn to instruct
him of the danger in which he might stand—and he
volunteered himself, that he would help deliver such
reports as might best deceive, that the High Priest
might chant to Sorgun these reports. I hear in his
voice that the man would help."

Kinch thought that folk sought to read emotion
and character in the face, while learning to shape
their own perhaps practicing before a mirror, that a
smile might convey love when none was felt, or a
frown suggest dismay when in truth a secret plan
went well. And Kinch was minded that men listened
less for fealty or deceit in the voice, whether that
voice was another's or their own. But Trajus heard
only voice. And just as he might hear someone

behind him or upon a distant stair that folk with
eyes had not a hint of, so Trajus heard somewhat of
the soul of those that he and Kinch would interview.

"What we most need," said Kinch, "is time.
Time to make shields and spears. And after we have
them, would help if we knew when Sorgun would
come, that we could have ready the farm lads and
the fishermen of Inkling." Since dawn ever rang in
the brisk fall air the bright rhythmic clanging of the
smithies' hammers as they drew ruddy iron into
spear tips. Kinch had seized ten score white ash
poles twice a man's length. The aged merchant that
had been Wirt's rival pled that a gentle of Firnis
had need of them for his pleasure garden, and
would pay well. "Sorgun will pay a higher price,"
said Kinch. Several of the poles already had sharp
heads.

But metal was ever the foremost hunger. Amid
Cook's maledictions and Maudie's tears, Kinch had
scavenged the kitchen of half its metal. Even Butler
must grumble that he lost several platters and a
caldron, for ever the smelter must be fed. Several
mirrors and brass inlays and ceremonial armor and
showy horse armor had also mingled their natures
with more karlish metal. And on the beach of the
fishing village south of the Cut lay the skewed
timbers of a southern bark, her metal stripped for
shield fronts.

"Sorgun," said Trajus, "will not come until the
harvest is most complete. But the High Priest and
his priests know that the wheat is scythed from the

fields. They hear the threshing and the millstones agrind. They see the grain sacks. And they must suppose much the same of Moor End, Mirdol, and Mittol, even unto the Eigin lands under Firnis. No tale of Novice Hind can change that."

"Nor," said Kinch, "can we hope to sorcel the priests of the Eye that they not see our weapon-forging. And we cannot make them believe that in our stave training we but play or prepare for the solstice festival."

"Most true," said Trajus. "But ever does rumor ride far when truth be his horse for much of the way. Ask this. What do we do that all must see?"

Kinch summed all in his mind as he stroked the great pard that purred in her dream. "The harvest is now complete save if one count milling as part of it. We make shields and spears far beyond our stock of horse. And to warlike exercise we daily put karls and farmers and townsfolk—even the fishermen of Inkling village and the sailors and porters and others of the docks."

"Right, my lord," said Trajus. "And from Sorgun's raid what changes that set folk agossip in the marketplace?"

"Elgar is dead. You are captain general. The Vicar everywhere pushes the work forward."

"No blushes, lad," said Trajus. "You are Lord of the Eigin line and the only one in the kingdom that was not made to forswear your name. Lothian mothers scare their children with talk of Eigin. And you

go about with the great pard that is the sign of your
house. The market gossip is of you."

"What may we make of that and the rest?"

"We," said Trajus with a laugh, "will mix the
truth that Sorgun's priests will see with what Sorgun
will believe—malice and overweening ambition. Well
he knows we have little more than six score horse.
He will have confidence that his several hundred
horsemen may with ease smash us in the open field,
and thus cleave the wheatlands with havoc. But we
are busy shield- and spear-making. And in war we
exercise farm lads and fishermen for whom we have
no horse. Sorgun may well suppose that we prepare
to do battle but not here and in the open field.
Perhaps the story will go round—like it has already—
that we will guard against an assault by sea. Sorgun
came that way by night and in small numbers just
now. The man is stubborn. What more like than
that he will come again by sea, but in the day with
great force?"

"Would be folly," said Kinch, "for him to forgo
his great advantage in horse. Can he believe we'd
be so foolish? And what matter if he did believe this
tale? Will just make him more hot to come on us by
land on horseback straightway before we stand ready."

"Come, Kinch," said Trajus, holding the ilgras
medallion close to his nose, that he might sniff it.
"Be not mulish. Sorgun will not ask himself whether
we shall be so foolish but whether you will be so.
You who he now must know are his ancient enemy
Eigin. Eigin whom he thought made nothing. Eigin

who most magical made nothing of his raid and strangled the Vicar's son. If Sorgun hears it put about that you build a small army to oppose a sea landing, and minded that the man who smashed his sword is no fool, he will ask himself what you secretly intend. What more like than that you will see to your ambition and revenge your house upon the King in Firnis?" Now Trajus held the milky white ilgras medallion to his ear.

"But," said Kinch, "however Sorgun does his arithmetick he would know that I would need twice the men and thrice the horse ere even I ride up through Moor End and Mittol to raise the country and invest Firnis."

Now Trajus made a pause in his reply. And he sucked his tongue, as one who would have the person who last spoke think more on what he had said. "Indeed that is the logick. So Sorgun knows you would need more men. Then you would send for them. And where would you send but to the ancient Eigin homelands south and west of Firnis?"

The great pard stirred and rolled her great gray-green head upon Kinch's thigh.

"Suppose this," said Trajus. "Suppose that aside from the great news that all goes forward in preparation for a sea assault, there is a small news. And the small news is that Hacmon and some horse of the garrison will go north on the great road toward Firnis. No reason given for this expedition save that Hacmon will bear messages and Southkirk's friendship and fealty to the King. The number that will go

with him will privily appear large. Perhaps three
score horse, though the public word will be a small
number. The one matter that shall be most clear
and public will be his leaving date. Perhaps a week
of days from now, when we will have our arms
ready. A day later we may call Hacmon's farmers
and Inkling's fishermen and the townsfolk to a harvest celebration. Doubt not that Sorgun will come
raiding the next dawn.

"And one matter more. The Novice Hind may
hear—perhaps from Wirt's young bride—that Wirt
and some others are engaged, most privily, in building a cage that will be borne upon a horse-pulled
cart."

"A cage?" said Kinch, who knew not what this
sudden turn in Trajus' sober propositions meant.
Now came Trajus' empty, grisly scarred sockets full
into Kinch's eyes.

"Sorgun now sees his ancient enemy Eigin in
Southkirk. And what can a cage be for but for the
great pard? And why would Hacmon go north now
except that he might raise the Eigin House lands in
your name? And what better earnest of your authority than that Hacmon bear with him the sign of your
house become flesh? Sorgun will come hot to
Southkirk like a lover to his mistress' bed."

Kinch coughed and sucked in air as one would
say something but has not yet the words. And Kinch
thought of his homelands and incontinently of Lady
Arlynn and he wished that his words might scurry
toward her as they might speed with an ilgras

medallion, and not merely by horse. And Kinch was minded to say that there was some wisdom in the Sorgun that Trajus limned for him. But Trajus, who now held the medallion close before his sockets, forestalled him.

"How like," said Trajus, "a mirror this is. I doubt not, as we concluded, that if one press it so that it warms and then chant those words, one's voice will travel far to Sorgun or some other. But it will carry a base voice as easy as a noble one, lies alike as truth. Will add not a whit to one's self as may a comrade or a lover. Will just make one's voice louder that folk may hear it afar. And it will make one's voice privy, that one may play sneak-in-the-night. We had best beware, my lord, that it not tempt us to the ways of Elgar and the High Priest."

Kinch, who had meant to talk of the great pard and other matters, was now caught in Trajus' thought. And he wondered at the medallion and even at the ilgras that composed its surface. For as Nim had said, ilgras was a most peculiar substance, that was incorruptible like other jewelstones, yet lacked their hardness. Ilgras was milkily soft like pine wood, yet it lacked the grain of wood, and it would neither rot nor rust. Though it burned in hot flame with a horrible tarish odor like a dead animal that had lain sealed in its own corruption for centuries. Trajus and he were agreed that the medallion was not made in Lothia but came from the Southern Empire or still more distant climes. The same might be true of the ilgras of which it was made.

"Worry not," said Trajus, "after either of your loves. For Hacmon will but circle back under cover of night, that he and his horse be ready to help against Sorgun. And if Lady Arlynn has gone from the place of seeing to Firnis, why sure it is that she will be safe there even if Sorgun and his horse win through to Mittol. And withal she is a better ambassador than gaunt Hacmon or even your pard."

The great pard, who was awake at Kinch's side and who knew her name, now barked a most friendly bark at Trajus, and rose up and stretched most mightily, and pulled up sod, kneading in the thin grass of the common yard with her foreclaws.

XX

Spreading his pinion feathers to cup the wind that
swept up to where the dawn sun lit the eastern face
of Rach Soturn Pikes, the raven rode the currents
high. As glass that reflects but does not discriminate,
the raven's iris made little of the distant movements
of horse on the edge of the southern fens. A half
mile below the Ham, an advance party of fifty
Lothians had been installed for a time. They had
seen or heard nothing from Southkirk Fort or town,
the more assured that the garrison was depleted and
the folk within in deepest sottish slumber. Behind
the fifty now paced forward some two hundred
horsemen, their dust making a low brownish mist
with the morning's moisture. Some sixty bowmen of
the Lothian mountain country rode in the van. But
the principal body carried longswords, some body
armor, round shields, and here and there a mace or

lance. Their horses moved with steady, heavy strides. At their head came huge Sorgun.

The raven followed from the sunny height how now below a half-dozen of lightly armed, black-clad horsemen sped forward across a shallow section of the Ham and wheeled round past Southkirk toward the signal crag. These horsemen left the view of Sorgun and his host as they wheeled. The raven saw them enter a grove of trees past the north meadow as they followed the path to the coastal ridge. They did not reappear. But soon a lad of Southkirk came from the grove and waved a large cloth at the bartizan of the northmost part of Southkirk Fort. On that bartizan sat Trajus. With him three runners, that might carry messages and be his eyes.

"Ho, Kinch," called Trajus through his leather speaking trumpet to where folk milled about in the common yard below. "We have ta'en their advance squad. They will not go bird-nesting on the signal peak." Kinch's hundred of the left stood ready with their door shields and long spears under the main gate. Most also had short swords or long knives. They were karls and fishermen, though Kinch had added a score of seasoned seamen who had fought with pirates. Next them below the gate were marshalled the fifty horse that remained of the garrison. By plan Hacmon's three score horse lay encamped just over a rise, a mile up the great southern road on the way north to Firnis. From there they could see the bartizan in which Trajus sat.

"Where is the main body?" shouted Kinch through

his cupped hands. Best not to show Southkirk's teeth over soon. But there were three shallows in the Ham this season and even a wall that moved would need some time material that it find position.

"The main horse," said Trajus, "pace now some two miles from the Ham. Some of the advance party move forward. You'd best begin. I will give the sign to the signal peak." Kinch doubted on past accounts whether much heed would be paid by Moor End, that sat some dozen miles straight across the moor wastes and a score of miles by the great road. Far more than doubtful distant smoke were needed to move them. But that they of Southkirk were ready for battle would be plain once his men went out from Southkirk's gate. And the smoke would speak clear enough to Hacmon.

Next to Kinch stood the Novice Hind, who had with the Armorer and some warriors arrested the High Priest in the hour past midnight, bringing him and his medallion most silently and carefully into Southkirk Fort. Hind had heard the High Priest talk to his ilgras medallion and soon heard him snoring. The Armorer was sure that the man slept deep when they burst in upon him. And both were definite that he touched not, nor spoke to his medallion before they ripped it from him. If Sorgun inquired, the High Priest's medallion might at best speak to Elgar's, for both medallions now lay alone upon the great table in the Vicar's study.

Kinch laughed and embraced the Novice and kissed him upon the lips, as he had embraced and

kissed last evening each man of the horsed garrison
and of the three hundreds that would be Southkirk's
wall. Kinch was ware now, as he was then, that men
would die with him this day and upon his orders.
And he knew not which was the arm and which the
sword, which the willed thought and which the form
material, but all went forward as flows a stream or
grows a tree or moves a sun across a sky.

And now the raven was joined by his mate and
they soared in a widening gyre, riding the sun-
warmed air. By their third sweep toward the river,
Kinch's wing was settled on the left, athwart the
shallow of the Ham that was nearest to Rach Soturn
Pikes. Here for a space the water would rise only
inches above a horse's hocks. Where the Vicar's
force assembled a hundred yards to the south the
shallow was less wide and deeper. The six score
whom Syljanus and the Armorer led had just come
without the gate. Kinch had waved the fifty horse to
the rear behind the Vicar. The horsemen would
suffice to stop a stray squad or help shore up a
crack in the line. But the brunt would be upon the
men of Southkirk on the ground, with shield and
long spear. And their line must hold, or buckle off
in measured curves, for but a few men on horse
could slaughter many on foot if they could come at
their backs or sides.

"A charge of horse," had said Trajus as they
shared a morning draught, "is a thing most terrifying.
But at the Ham they must slow to a trot and must
cross within a narrow span. I will wager that in all

their days they have not charged a phalanx in the field. Look, Kinch, look to your farm lads and fishermen and karls. They are used to horsed warriors who spend their lives at arms, horsed warriors who live upon the bounty of peasant and laborer: used to the fear of them. If you cannot hold them to it, the Lothians will do sportful slaughter with them."

When the raven and his mate gyred northwest this third time, they rode a warm current up along the road, for they knew that their meat would come later. Farther up that road the ravens' wide black eyes held Hacmon's sixty horse, settled in a grove below the rise that hid them from Sorgun. Most all in Hacmon's party looked to that upmost part of Southkirk Fort that peeped above the rise. All save the great pard that was most privily fiercely gnawing at the hempen rope that held shut her cage. And all there heard the distant muted thunder of the Lothian horse pillowed upon the indistinct roar of the dawn that ran between sea and mountain.

His own wing at ready, Kinch was now with the men of Syljanus and the Armorer. Kinch had no armor save Trajus' gray leather jerkin that held Imperial chain mail on its inner surface. He went from one small group of three or four men to another, clasping hand or touching shoulder. Ever he would share a jest or soldierly sentiment. And his face, under his bare blond hair, was ruddy and his blue eyes flashed.

"He is beautiful," said Syljanus in the Armorer's ear, as they watched Kinch's rapid progress, marked by a burst of laughter or a shout, through their lines. Since two hours before dawn, Syljanus had been checking shields and spears. Talking to such men of his who were awake, he had made sure that they understood what was needful. They should hide the length of their spears and lay their shields along the ground, that the Lothians not know until they charged that they would have to do with a wall and a wall with teeth. Syljanus knew he was here in Hacmon's stead and that that was why the solid Armorer stood at his side.

"Beautiful?" said the Armorer and he sucked between his teeth as one who will find some lost portion of his supper. "Lord," said the Armorer behind his hand, "the man has made me near believe that I shall see your farm lads and Southkirk's dockmen stand firm against a charge of seasoned Lothian horse. That miracle were beauty enough for me, though his face be warts and sties from ear to ear." The Armorer now gave a sober smile and looked Syljanus full in the face. "Has made a sea change in you, most certain."

And Syljanus turned red at this and laughed and said, "We have all had our lessons at stave-fighting."

Now were Sorgun and his horse settled to a stop some tenth part of a league away, while Sorgun looked first this way and then that along the low walls of shields and men that faced him from the other side of the Ham. Certain, the Southkirkers had put on some greater show of spirit than the past or the High Priest would suggest. That might be laid to the account of that comely snip of an Eigin popinjay that he even now spied pacing to their wing that was nearest the road and the foothills of Rach Soturn Pikes. But their short spears and shields made a low wall. And peasants and fishermen who might well help defend a fortress could not upon the ground face a charge of Lothian horse. Their small squadron of horse were easily put down. He might go forward now, with his present force. And the popinjay Eigin's position were most toothsome, for that way was by report most wide and shallow. Best crush that Eigin flea now if he were to stay in Firnis this time and rule rather than ravage.

"Styrboeren," Sorgun said to the tallest and darkest one of the three lieutenants that were near him, "take your fifty across the shallows into their northmost troop there. After you have cleaved through them, stand ready for their horse. And you, redhaired Herbrand, bring your men close behind him through the shallows, and pause not when Styrboeren wins through but come straight behind him to awe their horse. Last, I'll lead the rest of the sworders and Lars' bowmen to do slaughter from behind, and where flight takes them, of the men on the ground. Go." And he saw high above him in the endless blue two soot-black ravens that wheeled south toward the sea and Southkirk.

Now shouted from the bartizan, through his leathern trumpet, Trajus, who said, "We still see no carts or wagons." The voice carried to the Vicar's group and Kindrel the poet that was there shouted the message on to Kinch.

Kinch now stood close with his own line of sixty shields that would first lay Southkirk's destiny on the table. They were in the sandy sedge grass that lay moist on Ham's edge. He could smell the sap in the new-cut wood of the shields. Across the Ham Sorgun's corsairs came forward. Kinch held Scut's arm and saw Scut's door shield, laid horizontal, ahead. "Will you do this thing?" said Kinch and he looked in Scut's eye. "Will do it," said Scut. Butler stood behind him in the open pocket behind the shield line with a two-headed axe. So armed might he deal with the hocks of a horse that won through into the heart of the phalanx.

And now the fifty Lothians with tall dark Styrboeren began their trot toward the shallow of the Ham. Their hooves beat heavy and dull upon the dry turf. As they cleared the last of the bush, their trot then became soon a canter, slapping on the wetter ground and crackling on driftwood and twig, and ever rising in a mad rhythm. While behind them came red-haired Herbrand, whose troop was wont to give a peculiar battle cry somewhat like the shriek of a pig.

Kinch saw that but two of Styrboeren veterans had lowered lances, the rest with but longswords. He knew that one above in the bartizan would say this thing to Trajus. For ever had Trajus said, "If they bear many lances, I'll not wager a turnip for our chances." And then had Trajus said, "But they will not."

Now Kinch shouted that his men should raise their shields, to lock them one another and to the ground. And Kinch shouted that they should put forward their spears. With his word the long spears, that were the length of three men, swung to point forth some third of their length beyond the shields. Their nether end was dug in the earth of the pocket, their middle yoked through a shieldman's arm and the side of his door shield. Thus did Southkirk show her teeth.

Styrboeren's horse splashed in the Ham and each foreleg, from coronets through pasterns to knee, cleaved Ham water wake-winged like the prow of a galley. And surely this host bore down upon Kinch's hundred as might cleave a new-born ship whose chocks were hammered free and that rolled upon dockyard logs with massive and growing solidity into the sea.

A score of horse died in that charge, most who took the long spears in the breast or shoulder, slicing up to the withers. But one horse won through and that one riderless, so Butler seized its reins and found first employment for his fearsome axe in driving a stake in the ground that he might tether the horse. Kinch and the others who stood within the pocket had more bloody work for their weapons, for four of the Lothians were thrown forward over their horses and the shield wall, and three of these drew themselves upward with swords in their hands. But they found their longswords clumsy weapons when borne upon the ground. Shields and shortswords closed upon them.

In the shallows milled the two dozen that remained of Styrboeren's fifty, and three riderless horses milled with them. Sorgun stayed Herbrand from the charge, shouting brazen-voiced to Lars that his bowmen should loose some volleys. Kinch's shield line still showed straight as Kinch waved those in the open pocket under the shadow of the door shields. And the water in the shallows ran furrowed with red.

"Where are the carts?" muttered Trajus. He called Steward Duggin and he told him to fetch the two ilgras medallions from the Vicar's study table. And he told Duggin that he should bear the two medallions upon a plate as though they were rare tasties, and not for fingering. Settling back in his canvas chair once more, he called that the man who looked through one of the bartizan's crenels should continue his account of the movement of Sorgun's horse behind his screen of bowmen.

Styrboeren, Herbrand, Lars, and some others had been called to Sorgun's side. "No," said Sorgun and gave them a wolfish grin. "No, we shall smash them now. Nettlesome true it is that my first simple stroke has gone foul. Yet we have learned somewhat of the ground and of their mettle. They be but scrawny peasants and foul-smelling fishermen. Peasants and fishermen puffed up for the moment into the thought that they are men of war because an

hundred of them have stopped a dozen of horse that
came at their fortification whilst slowed by a wide
yet shallow moat. Let me school you how we'll slice
'em to 'umble pie."

The Steward Duggin brought the two ilgras medallions upon a silver tray. As the Steward neared him
upon the bartizan, Trajus could hear the soft rattle
of the medallions upon the silver tray. "Fear not,"
said Trajus, "for they hold no danger for you. They
are but speaking horns of a sort. Put the plate on
my lap." And Trajus put a medallion to his ear and
he pressed upon the ilgras surface in that way that
made it warm. But he also bade Steward to the wall,
that he might tell how he saw the Lothians dispose
themselves.

And now as the bowmen loosed a volley, the
remains of Styrboeren's fifty and Herbrand's men
swept downstream and made into the Ham as if to
charge just above the Vicar's position. But then, as
the lone fifty of Southkirk's horse came north around
the Vicar's foot, the Lothians winged smoothly south
and charged across the middling shallows toward
the shields where Syljanus and the Armorer commanded. The first half dozen that came upon those
shallows then stepped further south and into deeper
water. And Trajus' voice came through his trumpet
so those of Southkirk should keep their line close
together.

Now those who stood in the line that stood closest
to Fort Southkirk were moved to action. For they
saw these half-dozen horsemen seek to come across

the Ham still further south. And well they knew that should some body of horse pierce within their shield wall, they would be as the he porcupine whom the she lynx will spin upon his back that she come opening of his soft-furred unspeared belly. So these folk of the southmost portion of Syljanus' shield wall spread some yards to meet the half-dozen horse. Thus small spaces opened in the front line of their shields. And more substantial gaps were made in their second line, that was thinner and must stretch farther. Those who rushed forward did not see that the half-dozen horse who now struggled in water to their ribs were in themselves no threat. Dark Styrboeren and his thirty now cantered forward through the shallows onto the weakened line.

Styrboeren spurred forward his mighty black stallion that was already bloody upon his breast. As he reached the splayed shield line, he pivoted violently to the right upon the point of a spear that hit his saddle, and thus threw his horse upon several of the shields. The rest of his thirty began to storm forward by ones and twos to enter the breach. And Styrboeren stood upon two shields and hewed all about him with his longsword.

Now Syljanus and the Armorer set about to bring shieldmen and spears from the sides of their position, that they might close this wound in their line and make harmless the few horse that would already make their way over the breach that Styrboeren's dying stallion bridged. These Southkirkers were fearful. And they stood back and would not go

forward to plug the line. But at this instant came
forward motive new.

When the great pard had teethed through the
rope that wrapped her cage door, she slipped without her cage. She would avoid Hacmon's men so she
went west and south about her task. So soon she
came around a grassy butte north of Southkirk but a
few hundred yards from the battle, and she there
heard Trajus' voice when he shouted through his
trumpet.

To the back of Syljanus' lines thus came by
bounds majestic the great pard. And she moved as a
force spectral, for her pads sounded not upon the
grass and moss. She came just as Styrboeren's grim
horsemen began to breast those lines from the front.
Whether through inspiration or fear, the shieldmen
and spearmen of the line's nethers closed forward.
Wirt amongst them shouted *Eigin* and others took
up his chant. The gap was plugged and the two
horsemen in the pocket died, and brave Styrboeren
had a great spear wound in his thigh. And Styrboeren's men grabbed him up and bore him back
from the skirmish.

Above them Trajus heard, as he pressed the
medallions to his hairy ears, Sorgun's voice. And
Sorgun's voice said, "Tarry not and come forward,
for our losses will be less if we overawe them. And
damned be the carts!"

Now came Kinch to Syljanus and the Armorer,
for he had run toward them when the Lothians had
wheeled that way. The great pard barked to see

him. She leapt upon him and folded her forearms
and paws around his shoulders and neck, and purred
next his chest. And Kinch kissed her upon her
muzzle and then pushed her off that he might look
about him.

And Trajus called through his leather trumpet, "I
have called Hacmon and his men down. I've bidden
him to ride for your wing." Then Trajus paused to
pull his breath in and he continued. "But thou wilt
have to do with three hundred more. You've seen
but half their force. Three more troops will come.
And they are but a mile from the Ham."

The Steward Duggin, that had but minutes past
shown the flag that would tell Hacmon to come
forward, now told Trajus how these men strove upon
the water and field of Southkirk.

And now it became clear that the feint seaward
and Styrboeren's attack on Syljanus' men was in all
still another feint. Herbrand's men and such as
remained of Styrboeren's men now paced north along
the shore of the Ham. And they rode so to come
behind Sorgun's house troop of four score that galloped into the northmost shallows that led to Kinch's
men, to the shield line where first they had attacked.
While Kinch ran northward toward his men, they
raised their shields and put forward their long spears
as might a porcupine show his quality. But Sorgun,
who now rode in the van, did not lead his men
straight unto this hard place of Southkirk. For in the
first charge of the day Sorgun had seen that the

shallows had a narrow branch north when one had come halfway across the Ham.

Sorgun now led his house troop up this branch and they shouted a great shout as they went forward. Now it was clear to Kinch's men that they must move a portion of their line some score of yards up the Ham. So went forward the garrison lieutenant and Butler and Scut, and the northmost wing of Kinch's phalanx. But the door shields were heavy and the long spears unwieldy. As the phalanx opened so Lars' bowmen, who looked to this unfolding, loosed several volleys. And while the arrows lost much of their speed through the distance, several were wounded or struck, so that the confusion of heavy shields and awkward spears was made far worse.

Kinch, as his legs took him by the Vicar's position, yelled to the two score horse that stood there that they should go north to help close the gap. But Kinch could see, as he ran forward, that already a half-dozen Lothians had come through the short, rib-deep channel. They stood upon the bank streaming water, and a steam rose from them, for the heat of the horses' striving and the sharpness of the air. And though a score of Southkirk shieldmen were now but yards from them, Kinch knew all stood desperate.

Now one saw how awesome the advantage held by horsemen over men on the ground in disarray. For Sorgun and three others charged forward into the Southkirk score that were no line but a mess of shields, spears, and men. Awful was the trail of twelve hooves and three longswords through those twenty men of Southkirk.

And now indeed did the men of Kinch's phalanx stand open as the overturned porcupine to the lynx. For half of Sorgun's household company had now come across the Ham, and they readied themselves for Sorgun's order. Sorgun wheeled from his small slaughter and stood for twenty heartbeats before these men. His face was ruddy and his sword was adrip with blood and he chewed upon some strands of his dark blond hair. And then he gave a great shout and set them forward.

But now the two score Southkirk horse had come forward from the Vicar's position, so that Sorgun must first have to do with them. And behind them Kinch drew his men together, that shield and spear might form a regular wall from the bank of the Ham westward toward the great road. The shieldmen drank in Kinch's face as he went along the line, clasping shoulder and arm. He laughed with one and another and set all in readiness for the storm. And he saw not Scut or Butler.

Sorgun's veterans soon cut down and cast aside the small force of horse. But when they came upon the shield wall they slowed. For truly Lothian horse had already bled much upon these walls that day. And Sorgun, that was no mad waster of men, called his horsemen west along the shield line, that they might come around and to the tender backside of that line.

THE SWORD AND THE EYE   205

Now was seen the wisdom of Trajus. For gaunt
Hacmon and his sixty horse, that had set forth on
the signal from Southkirk's bartizan, had come down
the great southern road from their place of conceal-
ment. They threw themselves full onto Sorgun's household troops as those troops sought to come round the
shield line. And the air was full of clang of longsword
on shield and the shouts of men and the snorts and
screams of the horses. Ever in the fray rode grim-
faced Hacmon forward that he might come upon
Sorgun. And Hacmon shouted at Sorgun that he
should fight with him. But Sorgun brought his weary
veterans around him and gave ground slowly. And
Kinch, whose head was apound with blood, led the
left of his line around back toward the Ham, as
though he would trap his foe against the water.

When he told Trajus that Kinch would pull his
line round to catch Sorgun against the Ham, Steward Duggin spoke like one who cheers his runner in
the victory lap. Trajus was cold. For he knew that
Kinch and Hacmon were angry geese who chase a
bear cub into a cave, with no thought that they
might soon have to do with the embrace of the cub's
mother. For Herbrand's troop and Lars' bowmen
had come over the Ham behind Sorgun's household
horse. All these crossings and reinforcements had
Duggin's eyes seen and reported. But Duggin's voice,
that had but an hour earlier quavered at the Lothian
might, was now hoarse and afire with victory.

Trajus fancied that his ears could hear, through
the crash and patter of battle, the splash and whinny

of the first hundred of the Lothian afterguard, that came now across the Ham, a force fresh and grim and alike in number to all that Sorgun had yet put into the field. And Trajus was glad that he had ordered the Vicar and his phalanx to move with all speed to strengthen Kinch's left, while Syljanus and the Armorer and their men made their duty more deliberate along the bank of the Ham, that they might secure the watery flank and strengthen Kinch's right. For Trajus knew that they of Southkirk would now face the full bearish force of Lothia. Trajus said to himself in a mutter, "Now if only Eigin knows when to bend, that he husband their lives and his own." Trajus knew that all now would be soon resolved by sword and spear and shield, and horse and man. And he heard far above him the call of ravens.

Now that Sorgun saw that the first hundred of his afterguard had come over the Ham, and the rest well on their way, he no longer gave way to Hacmon and Kinch. Straightway he wheeled on Hacmon and shouted most fearsomely, "Now, dog, I'll teach thee war." And he gave Hacmon a great blow upon helm and shield that carried through to wound and bruise Hacmon's shoulder and throw him from his horse. Now Sorgun's household troop and Herbrand's horsemen all began to make their way forward and sought once more to come round the anchorless left of Kinch's line. And Lars' bowmen loosed several volleys into the openings in the shield line that Kinch had made through his rash move forward.

When Kinch saw Hacmon fall to earth, he shouted his men forward no more. And as he paused to send forward men to bring Hacmon from the stour, Kinch saw a yet more sober sight. For he saw the tangled, bloody heap of Scut and Butler where they had died some moments past when Sorgun had first won into a portion of the shield line. The blood ceased pounding in Kinch's ears. He saw that the fresh Lothian hundreds that Trajus had warned of were now mustered on this side of the Ham, ready to follow Sorgun and Herbrand round the shield line. And in that moment Kinch knew that his men would go down like wheat before the scythe if the Lothian horsemen made their way around.

So Kinch gave order that his left give way all compact and orderly, and bend back from the great southern road toward Southkirk. Now Kinch saw that the Vicar's men were pacing up with long spear and shield, that they might form a flank and back to Kinch's men, and so balk Sorgun from his slaughtering. In that instant Kinch saw that the Lothian horsemen were like to win the race, coming behind and into the soft belly of his position before the Vicar's men could join his left and form another wall to his fortress of shields. And seeing this, Kinch leapt upon the empty-saddled Lothian horse that Butler had tethered when the first Lothian charge broke. And, swinging his singing sword in great swathes, he rode straight through the mêlée toward Sorgun shouting, "I have supped your southlands

bride, my cuckold Sorgun, and your great pard is
my mate, so now I'll make thee all ways a capon."

Now Kinch was minded that he shouted these
words only in policy, that Sorgun might pause. But
Kinch was full of rage at himself for having so
exposed his men. So full of rage and apprehension
was he that in but heartbeats he had buckled the
shields of two Lothian horsemen, shattered the sword
of a third, and near struck off the head of a fourth,
or ever he came near Sorgun. And Sorgun, that was
caught by the words and face of this Eigin apparition,
did pause and traded several blows with Kinch.
Now did an arrow hit the thigh of Kinch's horse and
another the stifle, and the horse reared back, and
several Lothians strove at Kinch with their swords.
Kinch was fortunate that his horse now lunged clear
back toward the shield line, that he might rejoin his
men.

Kinch was thrown when the horse reared and stumbled at its wounds, and those of Southkirk pulled
him within their line. And when he stood again, he
shivered and gasped and paled as one who has just
won free of a cataleptic fever. The Novice Hind and
Wirt stood close, as though they would hold him
from falling but dared not to touch. Now looking on
the battle Kinch could see that in the moment while
his frenzy had held Sorgun's horsemen, the Vicar
and his hundred had quick marched to join the left
of his line. When now Sorgun and Herbrand and
their men continued their flanking ride, they found
but more shields and spears as the shield line

buckled off, circling round toward the men that Syljanus and the Armorer led.

And so the Lothians found themselves facing a fortress whose gates were shut. Nor were those men who rode with Sorgun and Herbrand now eager to assault these walls direct. When Sorgun saw that this was so, he snorted and muttered, "scrawny peasants and foul-smelling fishermen," and he wheeled and rode back to where his fresh troops were mustered and he led them twice against the shields and spears of Southkirk. But in this exercise the Lothian horse did but probe for gaps in the shield wall and none seemed eager like the berserker Styrboeren that had spurred his horse to make a bed of spears and shields in dying.

And Sorgun said to Herbrand, "These scum have cost me three score horse and a brave lieutenant. I would be a fool to waste a like number of picked men to bring full slaughter on these peasant fishermen."

Herbrand, that put both butcher bills higher still, said, "We have pushed them aside and the way is clear to Firnis."

"And I," said Sorgun, "must sell my men dear if I am to overawe them in Firnis and stay there with the kingdom entire the Price. The Eye knows that we'll not catch them asleep if we tarry here over long."

So the Lothian hundreds paced north up the great southern road, winding between the watery moors and Rach Soturn, that they might come through to

Moor End and the wheatfields by the next sun's dawn and to Firnis by its dusk. And the men of Southkirk cheered and shouted insults at this leave-taking.

When, in the still hot air of noon, Southkirk's burial party saw the smoke to the south where the Armorer burned Sorgun's carts, the two ravens were so belly-burst with eating that they might not make their way aloft but must hop away upon the ground from those who would clear their banquet table. And within Southkirk's great hall peasant and fishermen, heads high, ate with more leisure and less gluttony. But Kinch ran.

XXI

Kinch ran. He had settled into his pace as one who knows he must go a long course and must sell his strength slow and dear. By the noon sun he had been on the bog path for near two hours. His feet were bare of the buskins that he had worn in battle. Calloused well from his morning exercise and the stone and gravel of Southkirk, his feet felt yet no sore. In the steady swim of his pace his mind now held only the endless beat of heel, ball, and toes, heel, ball, and toes, and the rhythm of the great muscles of his thighs and calves, and arms and torso, that drove this solemn music. The grove where he had once come upon the Lady Arlynn was already some space behind him.

He had stripped off his battle harness even as the soldiery of Southkirk still gawked at the dust and echo of the departing Lothian horse: the Lothian horse that rode northwest along a winding road to the wheatlands and to the King's place in Firnis.

All Kinch wore now was a loincloth. That, and the light straps which held the singing sword comfortable upon his back that it might not hamper his pace. Novice Hind had fixed these straps while Kinch had converse with the Vicar. Hind had devised well, for Kinch felt no pinch from the sword, and if it sang, it was in full harmony with Kinch's strides. Kinch said to the Vicar that he should tell Trajus to listen to distant sounds most carefully at sun's down and rise. And Kinch told the Vicar that it was needful to hold their men at ready, for Sorgun might be repulsed before Firnis and turn back on Southkirk.

The Vicar looked a question at Kinch. "If," said the Vicar with a smile, "you were a raven, this were no difficult matter. You might fly up the great southern road above and beyond Sorgun to warn the farm towns and distant Firnis. But, Kinch, you are no raven and Southkirk has no winged horses."

"My lord," said Kinch and laughed. "The watery path across the moors to the wheatlands is no place for horse's hoofs. But it will bear a man this season. And the path is straight from here to Moor End." Kinch was minded of what Trajus had told him long ago, that the human frame was not fit for speed but for distance alone, and that the will could draw more from that frame than any goad from a horse.

The Vicar looked into the blue Eigin eyes. "What can you hope to do with the folk in Firnis?"

Kinch snorted.

"And what seals of authority can you use to force their attention?"

"The last two post riders," said Kinch, "carried my respects to my leman and kinsfolk. Perhaps they are prepared to make the way more nettlesome for Sorgun this time." Kinch embraced the Vicar. Then he said, "As earnest of my person and authority there is the singing sword, that has long been with the Eigin House." When the Vicar started at the name Eigin, Kinch caught his eyes and said, "If the singing sword fail, I can always show them my nose." And withal Kinch laughed in such a wise that the Vicar gave a great laugh too.

Ever more powerfully, as the beat of heel, ball, and toes, and heel, ball, and toes, ran on, Kinch felt that he ran as Master Nim had instructed him. Without thought, that he be only what he did. And he smelt the sweet boggy air and heard only his foot beats and the sudden calls of birds as he pursued the sun westward. The last that the Vicar had said was sober. "I tell you true, Kinch, that you have had a most famous victory."

"Trajus," said Kinch.

"Yes, Trajus," said Vicar, "and Hacmon and the garrison horsemen and our farm folk and docksmen and the fishermen of Inkling village and even the great pard that now pants at your feet—all have had a most famous victory. And might not a few most fleet of foot accompany you across the watery moors?

You need some force if only to awe brigands on the road."

"The brigands," said Kinch, "who prey upon the great southern road may murther a man or two, as they may one who would climb past their mountain lairs in the Soturns. But none travel the moor paths save kindling gatherers and shepherds seeking strays. And even an hundred runners would increase my force not a whit. For I will carry an alarm and the name of a great house, and that burden may one man bear as well as ten thousand."

The Vicar, that must not say the word Eigin on the King's command, now did most solemnly with his hands the sign of the Eigin House. Kinch put her collar upon the great pard that still panted at his feet. And he handed her leash to the Vicar, that Trajus and the Vicar might have care of her. "I have been," said Kinch, "your son in service if not in nature and now name material."

"Shush," said the Vicar. "I am already a Vicar once. Twice is no burden more. Though," said the Vicar, and he smiled through his kinky grizzled beard and looked circumspectly at the great pard, "I think I shall give your pet to Trajus' care. Her ivories may not dazzle him."

And still ever more powerfully, as ran on that beat of heel, ball, and toes, and heel, ball, and toes, Kinch felt that he ran unwilled and without reason. His mind held neither rein nor whip and but dreamed upon the saddle of the body. Even the thrice his face splashed cool in sweet water pools and his lips drank deep, this too was but dream. And he smelt the sweet boggy air and heard only his foot beats and sudden bird calls and the cricket buzz and vivet calls that were nature's evensong.

Kinch woke from his dream in the farm village of Moor End. He had come between two barns and several small farm houses. And he had somehow come to a stop where the moor path met the great southern road. His body felt the ground sway as if he had come ashore from a sea voyage. Three peasants were standing a few feet from him. They stared. Some women in brown homespun also gawked at him from the shelter of the large barn. More folk began to gather, for it was near to sunset, and the cows were milked and the fields empty. The tallest of the three peasants who stood before him sent another to get one who was named Grundrin.

The eldest woman, Marta, came from the barn with a large wooden dipper full of water. He still swayed and his eyes looked through the slack-jawed woman, whose cheeks had been burnished red through scores of years in the field. But she held the dipper to his crusted lips. "Drink, lad," she said. The sweet cool water was in his mouth and throat and some dribbled down his chin and chest.

Grundrin had white hair and a grizzled face and his left eye was gone and his brow scarred above it. His right eye was blue and gauzy and he looked with it first at Kinch's back, then side, and finally in his face. And Grundrin sniffed at Kinch and pointed at the handle of the singing sword that peeked from above Kinch's shoulder.

Kinch drew the sword from the harness and held the blade upon his palms. He stared at it and felt from a great distance the song of the sword through his palms and fingers. The sword cast the sun's red light here and there amid the farm folk.

Grundrin's single eye now was bright as he drank in the liquid surface of the blade. His solid, weathered hand went forward slow toward the blade. He did not touch but limned close the sparkle of its cutting edge, as one who assays the proportion and authority of an instrument. Now Grundrin's hand came still more slowly to trace the outline of Kinch's brow and nose and cheekbones. All were silent that watched Grundrin inspect the man. And all one might hear was the measured sound of Kinch's breath, that was still heavy with his run.

Now Grundrin stepped back and straightened, and his ancient frame put on the posture of a soldier to his captain. "My lord Eigin," said Grundrin. "Some saw smoke from Southkirk way this morning. Though often it happens so with no thing amiss."

Kinch had his voice now. He told folk that Sorgun and his horsemen would come in the morning. He bid them hide their hams and cheeses and cart away the grain and mill of the harvest, that Sorgun have little to burn.

Indeed after he had had some more water and some bread, Kinch found he had the strength to help unload some lofts. But when dark was full

come, Grundrin and Marta bore off Kinch to a pallet
in the large barn that was laid with fine linen from
the manor. Marta washed and then kneaded his feet
with goose grease. And Kinch slept as the dead of
Southkirk field until Grundrin woke him with the
sun.

Kinch gasped when he first put his feet upon the
road from Moor End to Mittol. But as the dawn grew
this pain faded alike with the ache in his knees. It
was soon midmorning. He saw in the distance before him the Mittol mill house. He heard the Severn
River that here crossed the great southern road and
that flowed west. And he knew that beyond the
ridge on the far side of the sweet-watered Severn,
there began the narrow road that led from Mittol to
the farmlands that were the home of the Eigin House.
This narrow road was called spring road because a
branch of it swung north to Firnis—though longer
than the main road it was used in late spring, when
the great southern road might be boggy, and water
blocked at Vivet Creek crossing.

His feet felt the timbers of Severn Bridge. And
then, as in a dream, he heard above the Severn's
gurgle, a voice most bright and musical.

"My lord," she said, for it was the Lady Arlynn,
"you come among your folk garbed most casual."

White-gowned and fawn-gray cloaked, she stood
with a brave-faced young gentle at the base of the
ridge that led off to the Eigin lands. As Kinch took
the last steps to her side, he heard the whinnies of
horse behind the ridge.

"Fie," she laughed and held him with her eyes that were as green pools in which he might drown. "Fie," she said and wrinkled her nose, "let one fetch water and perfume, for my lord is as passing casual in his smell as in his garb." And she laughed a laugh that foamed full of happiness. But now did she show herself not over delicate, for she took Kinch in her arms and kissed him firmly upon his lips. And while she still held him she whispered quietly in his ear.

"I bore your name to the Eigin lands. This here, Denheim is your second cousin through your mother's line, both good and brave. We have the six score horse that were needed. Many more would come but we lacked war horses. There are more horsemen to be had in the King's place in Firnis. Those of your house are still under oath against Eigin, as your cousin here, but now all know that you have not so sworn. Where are the Lothians? We have just seen smoke from Moor End."

"My lady," said Kinch aloud, "we did Sorgun's men much damage before Southkirk. Not the least that they left the field to us. They are now but few hours behind me. We will need more men than we might in past years, for he still has half a thousand horse, though some be war-shocked and weary and wounded."

"The black-cowled Priests of the Eye," she said, "say Sorgun will stay when next he comes to Firnis."

"And," said Kinch with a laugh that had some

tautness in it, "what does my lady Arlynn think of this prophesy?"

Her green eyes now inspected his blue most solemnly. "I think, Kinch that now must be Eigin, that you will come to Firnis and come before Sorgun." Their eyes held long and firm. And then the Lady Arlynn smiled and gestured to the ridge behind her where the Eigin horse snorted.

"And if," she said, "my master Derwent Eigin will bestir himself, our horse will come to Firnis before noon."

"The King?" said Kinch.

"The King," said Lady Arlynn.

"Most like you will find him at court, mistress," said the young Denheim.

And Kinch marked how Lady Arlynn laughed at this though he did not see the wit in it until they came to Firnis.

XXII

The King took the Lord Counselor's shot on the back hand, and drove it smoothly into the lower right back wall. Now Counselor John, who was fat though but thirty, must run forward and could not do more than hit the ball weakly and high against the back wall. He would that the hard-wrapped twine ball might carom from the ash-lathed ceiling so that the King might have a difficult hit. But the ball made but a gentle arc off the back wall. The King, grace girding his tall and ancient limbs, racqueted the ball sharply and low to the far left. The page called "score" from behind the screen before the bellows-breathing Lord John was halfway across the court.

Kinch looked through the screen at King Harold Torndol, fifth of his house to rule this Salian Kingdom. Though Southkirk's Vicar was but "Vicar" to the lips of all, this man was "King Harold" to

some and mayhap but "Harold" to an Eigin. The
King and Lord John wore plain, loose-fitted breeches
and singlets. But even in such garb the close-
cropped white-haired man had a regal stance and
manner. Kinch saw that Lord John did not lose in
policy, for though the King was twice his years, the
King ruled in this court by skill and strategy. Would
that he had ruled rather than reigned outside this
court, whose glass-smooth, oak-planked floor would
make shields for a troop and whose ceiling laths
would make spears for an army.

Kinch, Lady Arlynn, and young Denheim had put
the full force of their persons upon the Chamberlain,
that he let them come apace to audience with the
King. Still, the Chamberlain would not go into the
tennis court until this interval of the game go by.
Kinch was minded that this interruption were as
well to the advantage of Lord John, for his face was
flushed red and his clothes were dark with sweat.

King Harold blinked at Kinch as he came into
the court. Though the page had wrapped him in a
wondrous colored silk robe, the King seemed to
shrink and grow gray as Kinch walked to him.
"Now, young man," said the King, "what is this
pother about Sorgun and his Lothian thieves? If
there be need, we will pay the Price."

"The Price may be the Salian Kingdom," said
Kinch.

"You have been listening to those damnable black-
cowled Priests of the Eye. 'Shalt stay in Firnis
when next he comes,' indeed. Nonsense, he'll take

his bag of gold and leave us." But now the King saw
Kinch's face full and he spent some time inspecting
it. And now disappeared the watery look that had
been in his eye since he put by his racquet.

For a space of fifty heartbeats Kinch stood in the
King's curious gaze. Then Kinch took the singing
sword from his cloak and kneeled and laid the
naked blade upon his palms before his King. And
King Harold looked down in wonder upon that blade
and face.

As if there were no other in that chamber, the
King now most carefully and softly touched the
sword. "These," said the King to himself, "are
ancient things come alive once more." The King
most carefully and softly touched Kinch's brow and
nose. "And this is an Eigin captain general as we
had in ancient days."

Now in all this the King spoke in a distant voice
as one who dreams. But when the word Eigin left
his lips there was a stir in the chamber. Lord John,
the Chamberlain, and young Denheim visibly started
and stared at the King. And the King took in their
gaze.

"The King," he said to them, "cannot be bound
by his own laws. An Eigin he is and I will say his
name. It comes to me now that in centuries gone by
Firnis has always had an Eigin as its captain general and I am of a mind that it shall be so again."

Now the King bent down once more to Kinch,
that now must be Eigin, and said, "I will have you
be my general, Eigin. Will you be so?"

"Yes, my liege," said Kinch.

"Well, then, it is so," said the King. And Lord John and the Chamberlain threw up their hands. But the King glared at them and made them silent.

"What I have done, I have done," said the King. "This Eigin is now my general. And if the King says the word Eigin, it surely shall not be forbidden his people."

With this last sentence, the King's face lost its regal bearing and he giggled, as though he had done some joke. The King's eyes were watery once more and he blinked at those about him. "Enough," said the King, and his voice was that of a querulous and bewildered old man. "Enough of business. You, Derwent, Orthos, or whatever Eigin you are, go about your generaling. And I'll thank you that the rest of you leave this court, that Lord John and I may continue our racquets. Go!"

"Two men," said Kinch to Lady Arlynn as they came without the narrow, stone-walled corridor that led them from the King and his court into the dazzle of the midday sun. "Two men have recognized my sword and name and person. And I know not which pleased me more, nor which did me greater honor."

"My lord," said Lady Arlynn, "in my land it is said that honor is the harness of duty. And while I am not the cynic that says all must nap but lightly in the favor of kings, this King Harold seems most changeable. That Counselor, Lord John, gave an ill look when you were named captain general, and he was loath to continue the game. I am minded that you must still now be Kinch as well as Lord Derwent Eigin."

Kinch laughed and smiled most prettily into her grave face. "Will you," he said, "not let me stand still for but that moment needed that my eyes cease to dazzle at the sun?" And he took her in his arms, but not for over long.

For he knew that with the garrison horse and the Eigin raisings he had but half the Lothian force. And there were no time to make door shields and spears, and to instruct and courage and weld secure a phalanx of steady foot soldiers. But Kinch was minded that men might even this day display themselves with shield and spear, though they knew not their proper battle use.

XXIII

"The three medallions are alike as one thing seen three times," said Kinch in his throat.

"What says my lord?" said Lady Arlynn.

"Alike," said Kinch softly as he fingered what he had just ripped from the throat of the High Priest of the Eye in Firnis. "Alike as three buttons from the same mold—or mayhap still more perfect alike. They are no natural stones, as of the seashore or the hill, nor be they some hard fruit of a tree, or other thing once alive like teeth of the pigheaded shark. No, these things are molded, forged, sewn, cast, or otherwise turned out, and those who make them must make other such instruments." Kinch's eyes turned along the frontworks of the temple of the Eye to where Denheim and some guards held the High Priest.

"But the priests have these medallions and no

other such devices. And they have not the smithies
for making these medallions, nor have these priests
the way of smiths about them. So they have stolen
or bought them."

"Stolen?" said Lady Arlynn. "These priests do
have a thievish manner."

"Most true," said Kinch. "But one might reason
that those who made these voice casters would not
be easy prey. Whether stolen or bought, I am minded
that this priest will fear those who made these
instruments as might a wayward dog his master."

And now Kinch raised his voice and called to
young Denheim and said, "Bring me the High Priest."

When the plump, turkey-chinned priest was come,
his hands trussed behind, Kinch ordered all to go
aside some paces, that Kinch might have privy
converse with him. Kinch looked down at the medallion that he held in his right hand. And he thought
on what might be the manner of an outland trader
whose kin had made this instrument.

"How," said Kinch, "came you by this?" Kinch
saw sweat upon the priest's face, though the sun
was now but a red ball on the low western hills.

"My lord," said the High Priest, "it is but the
jewel that marks my office." And the High Priest
reached smoothly for the medallion but Kinch gave
him no with a small gesture of his left hand.

"It is," said the priest unctuously, "precious to
my soul and to the Eye. As ilgras it may fetch some
price in the market. But that is naught to me for
reasons spiritual. And a lord such as you might add

to his estate by taking our temple whole, but not through seizing this small bauble."

"How came you by this?" said Kinch. His voice was even and firm, and he was as one who will not hear a child's errant prattle but will simply put the question once more.

"My lord—" said the High Priest, kneading his hands together.

"Shush, man," said Kinch, "and do not play the fool. Why do you think I sent these gentle country folk away? Though if you will be foolish, I can have them back that they practice some local evil on you." And Kinch held the priest silent with his eyes.

"Priest," said Kinch, "your temple looks down an alley into the marshalling yard of Firnis. This afternoon you saw horsemen and foot soldiers come together there."

"True," said the priest.

"How many horsemen? And foot soldiers?"

"These things," said the priest, "have many seen. The garrison, which is an hundred and a dozen more, and the Eigin raisings. Some twelve score horsemen. They rode out through the high gate down the great southern road."

"And the foot soldiers?" said Kinch.

"More difficult to count," said the priest. "First the Eigin horse marshalled whole in the yard, where one might count them as sticks laid in a row. Then some several score of foot marched through the yard and out down to the high gate. They had shields near the height of a man, and long spears, the like in size I have never seen. And after they had gone by, the Eigin horse trotted off toward high gate, and then came another column of these strange foot soldiers and another until the garrison marshalled up to make the afterguard. Perhaps three hundred foot soldiers, perhaps an hundred more, for I saw them pass by in but dribbles of a score."

"And where," said Kinch, "did all these go?"

"Down the great southern road toward Vivet Creek and Mittol."

"By what token know you this?" said Kinch.

"As those," said the priest, "who will take the narrow spring road will go through the low gate, so those who will take the high will go down the southern road."

"But whither have these troops gone?" said Kinch.

The High Priest smiled at him. "You, my lord, will know this more than I."

"I am not your lord," said Kinch. "And whither have these troops gone? And why do you say Vivet Creek?"

"Lord," said the priest, "I can but tell the common tale. Even the ironmonger would admit that Vivet crossing would be the one place on the great southern road where shields might make a wall against horse."

And now Kinch raised his eyebrow and eased his posture and smiled at the priest. "Yes," said Kinch and then fingering the medallion he quickly added, "and that gossip was all our instruments heard when you made your report to this Sorgun on our voice caster here?"

"Yes, that—" said the turkey-chinned High Priest, and then he saw that place that he had been led to, but saw no other path to take, and the way harmless surely to the puzzlesome ways and strange purposes of this outlander.

"Our instruments," said Kinch, "heard your 'Firnis will hear thy will, O Lord,' and your small babble just repeated of local soldierly movement. Sirrah, we heard your drivel as far as the moon. Was that all?"

"Yes, that was all that there was to say."

"Save that Sorgun asked you to confirm that the great southern road had to be the road of these troops? And that Vivet crossing was some several miles from Firnis and the spring road to the south?"

"Yes, Lord. Sorgun has not close visited Firnis."

"Then," said Kinch as one who talks but idly. "Then you spoke through this medallion but moments after the last horse passed out the high gate?"

"Even so," said the priest.

This was an end for Kinch, and laughed that he here had read the sticks somewhat as might the Novice Hind. And the High Priest wondered that this strange outland Lord would go away after asking but small questions. But he was not wholly happy, for his medallion was not returned and he was clapped up under guard.

Kinch was minded that it was good that the temple of the Eye was some yards from the marshalling yard. A closer and more skeptic eye might have seen that the several hundred foot soldiers were but thirty palace warders who had not before carried such outsize shields and spears, but who must circle ten times through the yard with them. And Kinch knew that there was yet need that he be Kinch.

"Shall we," said Kinch when Lady Arlynn was come, "now seek to trouble Sorgun in the night on the spring road?"

XXIV

Now at its zenith, the gibbous moon cast milky light through the craggy indentations that were called the Claws. The spring road ran some several score of yards at the bottom of this fancied giant talon mark. Kinch was minded that that legendary raptor was gargantuan in both size and height. For the eight rocky, lichen-blackened cuts that formed the Claws went down to the road some scores of feet so sheer that they were but five horse-lengths across at the top and a good three horse-lengths at bottom. Here surely was a place where a few above might do great mischief to many below. And curious that he, who now commanded horsemen, should have no use for the horse who now were tethered north beyond the trees that they had felled across the rise of the Claws, the horse tethered there that their snorts and whinnies might not alarm the Lothians.

Kinch had started when the Lady Arlynn had shaken him from sleep. Though he had gone several times the circuit of his men and said some words with all, and seen that each had supply of darts and arrows and a mound of stones for hurtling down, yet Kinch could not put sleep by. So now he heard the clank and scrape of the approaching Lothians as a distant choir whose song he knew not.

And though indeed Kinch Eigin had placed his men with sober generalship, and was to give his shouted orders well in the mêlée, in after days Kinch could call from memory little of this midnight meeting. Little save the scattered array of large moonlit boulders that were to him as pebbles of ilgras, and the black men and black horses that spectral clambered here and back athwart these boulders. That and the horses' shrieks and the men's shouts and screams and the unrhythmed rock clatter and thud. That and the fathomless eyes that Lady Arlynn gave him after they looked down upon the scattering of still dark heaps upon the moonlit rock, and heard the ebbing noise of the Lothian retreat. That and the huge black image of Sorgun who had caught up the red-bearded, neck-arrowed Herbrand and held him safe upon his saddle, and that shouted up through Herbrand's blood before he wheeled away, "Eigin, know that I will have my hand intimate upon you before the next moon dies."

If truth be told, Kinch came but full awake when those sent scouting at dawn came before him. Footsore and numb where not aching, Kinch strove to

attend to the word of the chief of the three horsemen
from the Eigin lands.

"Yes, Lord Derwent, they rode near to Mittol,
where they made camp some halfway between our
midnight skirmish and the dawn. We watched them
from a sheltering crag. And this Lord Sorgun gathered them about him and told them they would go
up the great southern road in the morrow and invest
Firnis. And, lord, there were clear more than four
hundred men, though there were many asleep or
whispering amongst themselves when Sorgun spoke.
And, having spoke, Sorgun took off the wounded,
red-bearded officer to his tent and slept deep."

"But," said Kinch, "with the dawn—?"

"My lord," said the man, "with the first graying,
we could see clear why there had been more rustlings than sleeping men might make. For the Lothians had most stolen off by dozens and scores, leading
their horses. And they had even taken off their
tents, so that when the last few score went off in the
full dawn, they left great Sorgun's tent alone in the
field. Alone there with his great black stallion that
bit the straggler who would bear him off."

"And then?" said Kinch.

"After waiting for a time, I sent two to ride back
to my lord with these events. But hardly had I sent
them than I saw bare-chested Sorgun come without
his tent, cradling the dead red-bearded officer and
holding him up, as one might who would show an
object honored to the world. But then Sorgun slowly
looked about him and turned widdershins in full

circle, and knew he was alone. Now Sorgun put the
dead all careful in his tent, and blew up the ash-
cloaked embers of the fire and lit the several sides
of his tent, and then took saddle on his black war
horse and rode all gravely south with the smoke. So
I galloped back and rejoined my messengers ere
ever they reached you at the Claws."

Kinch sent all forth save the Lady Arlynn and he
pressed upon and talked into the High Priest's
medallion. "Trajus," he said, "Sorgun's horsemen
have had a surfeit of battle and have left Sorgun in
the night, his chief lieutenants now dead, brave
Styrboeren from his wounds before Southkirk, Lars
in the stour last midnight, and Herbrand dead from
his wounds this dawning. So the Lothian horse will
most like come to Southkirk disorderly, though their
numbers will still be many. I am minded that shields
interlocked may net us a large catch before this day
goes down."

Now he put the medallion to his ear that he might
listen. But though Kinch heard enough of Trajus'
voice to know that Trajus had heard him, yet he could
not understand what Trajus said. So Kinch said,
"Send horsemen up the great southern road to tell
me when the skirmish is resolved. And trouble not
to speak more into your medallion, for your voice
sounds soft and hoarse and echoes through an hundred branching vessels and I cannot parse it into
words."

Kinch smiled a lean smile as he turned to the
Lady Arlynn. "Perhaps our voices go through these

vessels by such different paths that Trajus' voice
has become but a blur. These jewels are like unto
mirrors, for they make but copies whether these be
sharp or dim. They will speak to anyone that listens.
And they have little character, for they will copy
evil alike indifferent with good. And besides I doubt
not that these vessels may give report to other
portals."

"I am minded," said Lady Arlynn, "that Trajus
can hear a sentence where one with sight might hear
but a sound."

XXV

And as that day went on to afternoon, oft Kinch had to feel that the voices of those that rode with him were hoarse and soft and came to his ear through an hundred vessels. Well it was that the Lady Arlynn rode close at his side as their party went careful down the balance of the spring road and from there east through stubbled wheatfields to Mittol and southeast to Moor End. The sight of Grundrin in the road at Moor End finally roused him out of his nightmarish half sleep. That and that Grundrin called out that there was dust visible from the curves of the road beyond, dust that was a scant half mile as might fly the raven but a good mile for approaching horse.

Now Lady Arlynn called out that she heard hoofbeats. All soon heard, and looked down an hundred yards where the road disappeared into rock

ridge and scrub pine, that above one could see
Rach Soturn in the distance, its upper bastions and
peak bright and valleys dark with the late day sun.
And Lady Arlynn called out that she heard cart
wheels.

Came a horseman that wore a garrison cloak of
Southkirk. He spurred up his mount and swerved to
a fast halt next Kinch and leapt from his horse and
saluted. Now Kinch saw that this was Wirt, and he
heard the horse's heavy breath, and he waited that
Wirt speak.

"Lord Kinch," blurted Wirt, and Kinch smiled
that Wirt knew not how to address this kitchen karl
who was now also master. "Lord Kinch, we have
routed them. Most are Southkirk's prisoners, a pal-
try score got by, and but a dozen Lothian dead and
less of Southkirk." Once started, his words tumbled
out, as though Wirt would give the news before Lord
Hacmon and the other riders and the cart should
come.

"Trajus," said gaunt Hacmon, "has set the Lothian prisoners to what he calls honest karlish labor.
Presently an hundred are cleaning and resodding
the scum yard, under the eye of the Armorer. The
kitchen has several score scouring and scrubbing,
culling and cooping, emptying the ash pit and making soap. And for the balance there is muck-raking
the stables."

Hacmon now smiled large at Kinch and Lady
Arlynn, and gave a great laugh, and said, "Trajus
claims Kinch here as his proof that this karlish

labor will reform these Lothians, but withal will keep them from mischief while we decide what to do with them."

And now Lady Arlynn, that saw the cart come up, turned to Kinch and said, "How thoughtful of Trajus who sees to your happiness in great things, that he cast down your enemies, and alike even in small, that he send your favoritest animal to your side to comfort and delight you." For she saw the great pard in the cage that sat upon the cart, and now all might hear the joyful barking that the pard put on.

"No, beauteous lady," said Hacmon. "It had much less of grace in the intention, for the great pard yowled most abominably for her master Kinch, and those in Fortress Southkirk have had but little sleep these past two nights."

And after Kinch had loosed the great pard and hugged and petted and made much of her, he asked Hacmon for news of Sorgun.

"He is not prisoner, nor dead before Southkirk," said gaunt Hacmon. "And I will swear he was not among those who slipped past our net."

Now Wirt, that had stood by in silence, made to speak. "The great black stallion," he said.

"Yes, Wirt," said Hacmon. "I give you, Kinch, my lord Eigin, a mystery. We passed a great war stallion near the roadside some two leagues back, where the foothills of Rach Soturn have their beginning. And this great stallion was like unto that Sorgun rode in the great battle two days past, and it was dead. But I did not stop, for Trajus bid me to ride straight to you and he was right."

"It was," said Wirt, "it was hamstrung."

There was a silence. Then Kinch turned to Lady Arlynn, young Denheim, and Lord Hacmon. And he said, "Perhaps you might make what you can of Moor End's hospitality for the night. The day is dying and Firnis and Southkirk both be too far. Grundrin here will give you shelter, albeit rude, and I doubt not he and Marta will pluck out some seasonable food from all we hid when last I was here."

"And you, my lord?" said Lady Arlynn.

"I will exercise the great pard and may be find out a thing or two," said Kinch and he mounted his horse and made as if to ride south. For all that they might protest Kinch was like stone, save that he would, at Lady Arlynn's bidding, take an escort of four horsemen. Soon these four horsemen and Kinch rode off south along the great southern road. And they rode slowly, for the great pard like all cats could catch any creature within several body lengths but could not go the longer pace save in a gentle lope, and withal Kinch was in a study and would ride in measured pace.

And the escort came back some two hours hence, with the fullness of nightfall, but Kinch and Kinch's chestnut horse and the great pard did not return with them.

XXVI

The horse was dead, and the painful message of his hooves in the roadside dust was writ but moments past. Some villain had sliced just above the hocks in the legs that bent under the belly in the midst of this confusion of wondrous muscled but cooling flesh, and the great blackish lips hung open round the brown-lined teeth where foam and blood consorted. The olive-dun cat that was the great pard sniffed careful at this and then looked big-eyed at Kinch, and at the crushed scrub and broken bracken above and behind the horse. There was no sound. Kinch Lord Eigin commanded the escort away. And he tethered his chestnut horse, and he and the great pard essayed the way marked.

And they came upon a clearing made by scrub pine cupped against a white stone face, a face on whose upper reaches the sun's last rays lanced red and golden.

Lips opened and they mouthed the name of Kinch's town, but they hissed it "South—kirk" rather than "Sow—erk," and they hissed it not in policy but in pain. "Southkirk, what shall I call you, Eigin lord? Southkirk that has come for me, I foresaw your coming, for the lion ever follows the hyenas." Sorgun coughed bubbly and spat blood.

Sorgun's back was on the white stone wall, a brass-bossed, black-stained leathern bundle cast against this milk gray, fire-topped frame. Sprawled here and there before him five men of the mountains; two, heads akilter, along the scrubby path into the sward, three cupped round Sorgun's legs as and-irons round a hearth. In all, great Sorgun was companied well for dark journeys, as some ancient barbarian monarch whose household would join his death. Mayhap as such a lord, great Sorgun's hands held his longsword. But he was not dead. And the sword pointed most steady at Kinch. "Come at me," said Sorgun, "for I must not die of the cuts of brigands." Kinch was silent.

"Hah," said Sorgun, "I see that you have brought your house cat, Eigin Southkirk. Will you let her sup on these or will she wait for my more lordly meat?" For Sorgun and the great pard now eyed each other. Now Sorgun would heave himself up and forward from the wall. But there was great pain in the effort and after the space of an hundred heartbeats, Sorgun fell back against his stone seat.

Now did Kinch sit across the clearing from Sorgun, his back against a tree's elbow, and soon came the great pard, that put her head upon Kinch's knee and was soon in a nap. Though eye glinted across at eye, the twain did not speak again until the near-full moon rose high into the night sky.

When the voice came again it was no hiss but clear and resonant and strangely distant. "How guessed you that I would take the spring road into Firnis?"

Kinch took the medallion from his cloak and held it up. "I knew that the High Priest of Firnis would use this instrument to make report to you. So I set my foot soldiers and horsemen to walk about where the High Priest might see them and then had them march off as those who would take the south road. This priest made due report to you of this. And we circled round and awaited your force in the Claws."

Sorgun had pulled his own medallion from his throat. "This?" he said.

"Even so," said Kinch.

Sorgun put his medallion between his grinders and bit down upon it. There was a dull crunch as though Sorgun bit a large unripe nut. The fruit was ill tasting, for Sorgun spat it out, saying, "Damned sulphrous earth and putrid vinegars." Sorgun spat several times more, saying, "I had always thought them poisonous priestly baubles. And they have no more character than a mirror." Now Sorgun's sword was down, and he waved that Kinch might move closer.

"The snivel and simper of the priests came through this instrument. News, gossip, moans and chants, lies and truths. Like a mirror or a dock whore it will take all the same. And the pig-weasel priests these instruments spawned were worse like the sons of whores. There was no wisdom and much of karlish thievery in these priests."

"So then," said Kinch, "the priests did not make these instruments, nor did their fathers?"

"Nor even," said Sorgun sourly, "nor even their fathers' fathers, nor any of their kin or kind—nor ours nor any natural to our climes or the Southern Empire. 'Steal a strange magic,' is what my father said when the Eye priests once again did some mean self-befouling stupidness. Some several score of years ago the priests stole these instruments from some outland tradesmen and travelers. Or, as my father had it, these stolen magical instruments, they gathered priests."

" 'What the pedant calls grammarye and the vulgar calls magic,' " said Kinch more to himself than to Sorgun.

"What says my lord?" said Sorgun.

"The memory comes to me," said Kinch, "of what my mother said respecting what is commonly called magic. She said there were four kinds and that none were magical in truth." And Kinch's words became distant, dreamy, and higher in pitch, as one who captures olden memories entire even in the voice of time past.

" 'The first kind is the self-knowledge that you will search for in a place of seeing. And that is a way most hard, for you will lose your own self in it. Another kind, a darker side of self, is the strengthening of the will within. Folk often use keepsakes or dolls or symbols in this exercise of will and these objects, though they have no power of their own, may serve to strengthen the will. Yet a third kind arises when priests use the fear of such objects and other sorts of sleight of hand to make their victims fearful or credulous or to work some other way with them. And a final kind is the use of certain leaves, flowers, mushrooms, and the like, that will relieve illness or give endurance or vision or some other weal or woe, and this most material kind is not like to the others though the herbalist will often add some chanting incantation or some smoky signs to her dosage.' "

"Your mother," said Sorgun, "was most wise. Like as not she would have said that the priest's magic was of this fourth sort. Though a crafted device and not a poisonous plant."

Now Sorgun fell coughing once more, but weaker than before. After a time he said, "I should have raised more horses." But he would say no more. And there was silence.

The night grew cooler and Sorgun's face whiter. Now there were beads of sweat upon his brow as he did war with pain, and his sword lay loosely in his great hands. Kinch dragged the brigand bodies aside into a stony pocket. He and the pard went to a nearby spring, that Kinch might wash and both drink. Kinch soaked a cloth in the cool water, that he might lay it upon Sorgun's forehead. And as forsworn Sorgun's hand came intimate upon his in the moonlight, but the grasp was weak.

When came the hour of the wolf, great Sorgun was overcome with pain and called out in a thin yet desperate, petulant voice, "Oh, sing for me, sing for me, boy, for my thought is cloudy troubled and the pain bites hard. Sing."

And so awful was Sorgun's voice that after a time Kinch sang that song that Kindrel had sung that night before the battle upon the Ham, but three nights past.

There were three ravens sat on a tree,
    Downe a downe, hay down, hay down
There were three ravens sat on a tree,
    With a downe
There were three ravens sat on a tree,
They were as black as they might be.
    With a downe derrie, derrie, downe, downe

Kinch stopped but Sorgun bid him sing on. And Kinch went on, giving the repetitions and refrains while Sorgun died.

The one of them said to his mate,
"Where shall we our breakfast take?"

"Down in yonder green field,
There lies a knight slain under his shield.

"His hounds they lie down at his feet,
So well they can their master keep.

"His hawks they fly so eagerly,

There's no fowl dare him come nigh."

The great pard now stirred with the first twitter of
the birds. And Kinch saw no movement in that great
black figure but he would finish the song.

Down there comes a fallow doe,
As great with young as she might goe.

She lift up his bloody head,
And kist his wounds that were so red.

She got him up upon her backe,
And carried him to earthen lake.

God send every gentleman,
Such hawks, such hounds, and such a leman.

When the sun was enough that one could see
clear and not stumble upon a path, Kinch took

down Sorgun's sword and tethered it and the singing
sword to the pommel of his horse. He returned to
the clearing where the great pard lay gracefully at
dead Sorgun's feet. Now he must push his right
shoulder firm into the lower ribs, grapple in with his
right hand and arm under the upper thighs, that he
might heave Sorgun's middle athwart his shoulders,
bearing up the bearish weight with the main strength
of his calves and thighs and knees. Somehow the
matter was done and Sorgun's body hung over the
chestnut horse. Through the new day Kinch and the
great pard walked to Firnis, leading the chestnut
horse. The Lady Arlynn and the rest joined their
party at Moor End. Even the King came with the
sunset to Firnis' principal burying yard, there to see
that Kinch did ensure, even onto his own use of the
shovel, that Sorgun would stay when he had come to
Firnis.

After the great noonday meal, celebrating the
end of the Year of the Vivet and the beginning
of the Year of the Pard, Lord Eigin and his
special party retired to Southkirk's great aftergallery
chamber, whose rock walls were still white from
the Lothian scourers of three moons ago, a place
where one might sip some final draught and enjoy
the solstice sun's ruddy evening face. Kinch and
the Lady Arlynn stood within the gallery itself.
There Arlynn instructed him with a brassy instrument from the south that might measure the angle

on the plane of the ecliptic of the sun or some
more humble star. Near the fireplace at riddles
sat Trajus, Hacmon, the Vicar, the Lady Edwina
that was Kinch's mother, and Master Nim, come
from Rach Nord for this season to Southkirk, like
the Lady Edwina from the Anticore convent north
of Firnis.

The Master Nim had not reclaimed the name of
Eigin, for he held that if he had sworn to the King
to renounce the name, he would not cast aside his
oath nor his name Nim, until the King saw fit to
swear him new to the name Eigin. "If I am," said
Master Nim, "once more Eigin tomorrow, perhaps
we will politicly baptize me Nim the day after, or a
worse name, 'til I be a bric-a-brac of titles. These
name swearings are acts of great seriousness not
lightly entered upon."

Kinch thought of the medallion still within his
cloak. Could a mere object such as this or a raven
or a tree be bad or good? As Nim was wont to say
one can take only so much instruction from indifferent nature. But if there were no good or bad in
nature, Kinch was minded, then there could be no
good and bad among men and women. There must
be something to what one says and does that is
constant, though we cast our voice or our image or
our body even to the distant stars. There must be
something constant, some natural commons of truth
and nobility, or the distance is not worth the fare—
and that creature made mutant who makes the

journey. Still, no other way was there, thought Kinch. The pard must look to the rustlings in the next bush and so too must we, however farther we then may someday see.

FRED SABERHAGEN

GORDON R. DICKSON

- [ ] 53567-7   Hoka! (with Poul Anderson) $2.75
  53568-5   Canada $3.25

- [ ] 48537-9   Sleepwalker's World $2.50

- [ ] 48580-8   The Outposter $2.95

- [ ] 48525-5   Planet Run $2.75
                  with Keith Laumer

- [ ] 48556-5   The Pritcher Mass $2.75

- [ ] 48576-X   The Man From Earth $2.95

- [ ] 53562-6   The Last Master $2.95
  53563-4   Canada $3.50

HARRY HARRISON

☐	48505-0	A Transatlantic Tunnel, Hurrah!	$2.50
☐	48540-9	The Jupiter Plague	$2.95
☐	48565-4	Planet of the Damned	$2.95
☐	48557-3	Planet of No Return	$2.75
☐	48031-8	The QE2 Is Missing	$2.95
☐	48554-9	A Rebel in Time	$3.50

NEXT STOP:
SPACE STATION

". . . I am directing NASA to develop a permanently manned Space Station, and to do it within a decade." . . . President Ronald Reagan, State of the Union message, January 25, 1984.

Are you a person of vision? Are you excited about this next new stepping stone in mankind's future? Did you know that there is a magazine that covers these developments better than any other? Did you know that there is a non-profit public interest organization, founded by famed space pioneer Dr. Wernher von Braun, that actively supports all aspects of a strong U.S. space program? That organization is the NATIONAL SPACE INSTITUTE. If you're a member, here's what you'll get:

- 12 big issues of Space World magazine. Tops in the field. Follow the political, social and technological aspects of all Space Station developments—and all other space exploration and development too!
- VIP package tours to Kennedy Space Center to watch a Space Shuttle launch—the thrill of a lifetime!
- Regional meetings and workshops—get to meet an astronaut!
- Exclusive Space Hotline and Dial-A-Shuttle services.
- Discounts on valuable space merchandise and books.
- and much, much more!

So if you are that person of vision, your eyes upon the future, excited about the adventure of space exploration, let us send you more information on how to join the NSI. Just fill in your name and address and our packet will be on its way. AND, we'll send you a FREE Space Shuttle Launch Schedule which is yours to keep whatever you decide to do!

- -

Name _____

Address _____

City, State, & Zip_____

NATIONAL SPACE INSTITUTE
West Wing Suite 203
600 Maryland Avenue. S.W.
Washington, D.C. 20024
(202) 484-1111